The Sorcerer of the Stars

Adventures in Reason

Kris Langman

Post Hoc Publishing

The Sorcerer of the Stars

Print Edition
Post Hoc Publishing

Chapter One

Homecoming

"EVERYONE HOLD ON tight!" Nikki yelled, wiping the sweat off her face. The time had come. She couldn't avoid it any longer. They were approaching the harbor at ImpHaven and she was going to have to turn Griff's ship.

Everyone ran to the railings and wrapped their arms around the stout wooden posts surrounding the deck. Nikki checked the wind direction again. The wind was coming over the bow and the sail was luffing as the huge ship threatened to go into irons. If that happened the sail would be useless and they'd be dead in the water. She knew how to get a small dinghy out of irons. You just pushed on the boom and sculled the tiller back and forth until you got the sail back to a close-haul position. But with such a huge ship they couldn't possibly move the boom by hand.

Normally she would have tried to tack, but there wasn't enough wind. Tacking even a small sailboat required a fair amount of wind. Attempting to tack without enough wind would get the ship stuck in the no-go-zone, the area between the ten o'clock and two o'clock positions off the bow. Her only option was to try and ease the ship into a beam reach, with the wind coming over the side of the ship at the three o'clock position. That maneuver didn't require as much wind. Nikki glanced nervously at the sandy hills of the coastline.

They'd left the Prince's dock in Kingston on a run, with a strong wind coming over the stern and blowing them straight out to sea. But during the night they'd slowly been blown closer and closer to the shore. She could now see the outskirts of ImpHaven and its cottages dotting the cliffs. Tiny white houses with thatched roofs. A line of windmills along the cliff top. A broad green river flowing into the ocean through two breakwaters made of rough boulders. Ships docked at a line of wooden piers just inside the breakwaters.

Nikki felt her stomach churn at the thought of having to navigate the narrow gap between the two breakwaters. She just couldn't do it. She wasn't skilled enough to perform such delicate maneuvers with such a large ship. Not to mention trying to dock it at one of the piers if she made it through the breakwaters without crashing. No, the beach was a better option. It was a long sandy beach just below the cliffs, and it was right off their port side. The ship might founder in the shallows as it beached, but that was better than crashing into the rocks of the breakwaters.

Nikki took a deep breath. She had to turn now, before the beach ended and the ship reached the first breakwater. She slowly turned the ship's wheel to the right, watching the mainsail closely. It flapped in the breeze, then the trailing edge of it caught the wind and the boom creaked as the ship slowly turned toward the shore. Nikki straightened out the tiller as the bow of the ship crashed through the first line of waves rolling toward the beach. Geysers of spray shot up from the bow.

"Darius! Fuzz!" she shouted. "Bring down the mainsail! Now! Cut the ropes if you have to!"

Darius the stonemason ran forward and slashed with his knife at the nearest rope attached to the mainsail. Fuzz waved at the youngest imps onboard and they swarmed up the rope ladders swinging from the mast and untied every rope they could reach.

The huge billowing mainsail slowly collapsed, like a balloon with a puncture, until it hung limply from the boom.

Nikki looked frantically from the mainsail to the shore. The ship was slowing now that the sail was down, but it still had too much momentum. The beach was approaching fast. "Darius!" she shouted, "See if you can drop the anchor! We need to slow down!"

Darius ran to the winch in the bow which controlled the ship's huge iron anchor. His heavy shoulders strained as he turned the handle of the winch. A creaking rasp sounded above the crashing of the waves as the anchor chain slowly revolved. Seconds later the ship gave a sudden jolt as the anchor caught on the seabed.

As Nikki suspected, the anchor didn't stop the ship. They were moving too fast. But the dragging anchor helped slow them down. The only thing left to do was to keep the bow headed directly toward the beach. Coming in broadside would tip the ship over on its side, but if she could bring it in straight they might be able to beach without tipping over. She tried not to picture what would happen if someone fell overboard and the huge ship crashed down on top of them.

Nikki tightened her grip on the wheel. "Darius! Fuzz! Everyone back to the rail! Hold on!"

The ship crashed through line after line of waves, slowing a little each time. Then they were through the last line of waves and Nikki felt a shudder as the keel scraped against the sandy bottom. The ship rocked and bucked like a bronco, but it stayed upright. Nikki thought they were home free until suddenly the rudder caught against the seabed and the ship tilted precariously to starboard. She struggled with all her might to straighten the wheel, but it was no use.

"Darius!" she yelled. "Come take the wheel!"

The stonemason staggered across the tilting deck, nearly falling on top of her as he reached the wheel.

"Turn the wheel to the right!" Nikki shouted. "We need to straighten out our approach!"

The stonemason threw his weight against the wheel, straining to turn it. The ship continued to list to starboard. Barrels started rolling across the deck, slamming into the imps clinging to the starboard railing. But then a stray wave lifted the ship off the seabed for a brief second. Darius turned the wheel and the bow straightened. The ship righted itself and headed straight for the beach. Their speed slowed and the ship slowly ground to a halt, its bow on the dry sand and its stern gently rocking in the shallows.

Nikki sank to her knees in a puddle of sweat.

"Miss, you did it!" cried Athena, running up to Nikki and throwing her tiny arms around her. "You have gotten us safely to ImpHaven."

Nikki sat watching her hands shake as Darius threw a rope ladder over the side and the imps swarmed down to the golden sands of the beach. She felt like she was going to be sick. Cation was mewling loudly from inside the rucksack on her back.

"Here," said Linnea, kneeling down beside Nikki and digging into the bag of herbs hanging from her shoulder. "Valerian root. Chew it. It tastes awful but it will calm you down a bit." She gently removed Nikki's rucksack, which was now growling, and put it on her own back.

Nikki took the woody, gnarled root and cautiously nibbled it. "Ugh. It tastes like old bowling shoes."

"What are bowling shoes?" asked Linnea.

"Never mind," said Nikki. She slowly got to her feet. Her knees shook as she tottered to the side of the ship and hoisted herself over the railing. She climbed down the rope ladder like an old woman with arthritis. She splashed through the jade-green water and plunked down on the sandy beach, lying back and crossing her arms over her eyes to hide them from the bright sun. She'd been in more than a few tight spots on her adventures in the Realm of Reason, but sailing Griff's ship was the worst so far. So many lives had been in her hands.

It had been too much responsibility. Now she knew how airline pilots felt.

"Come on," said Gwen, sitting down on the sand beside her. "It wasn't that bad. You got us here safely, didn't you?"

Nikki didn't answer. She was wrestling with an overwhelming desire to rush back to the portal near Castle Cogent. To the gateway between the Realm of Reason and her own world. She wanted to see her Mom again. She wanted to go back to being an ordinary student at Westlake High School. She even missed Tina, the snarky captain of the Westlake debate team. The problems facing the Realm of Reason seemed to grow worse with each passing day and she suddenly didn't feel capable of coping with any of it. Not with Rufius, the wannabe-dictator. Not with Avaricious and Fortuna and their greedy plans which got people killed. Not with the Knights of the Iron Fist who were charging around in their steel-plated armor, bullying and harassing the citizens of the Realm. And not with the plight of the imps, who were being forced out of their homes by nasty people who didn't want them around.

Nikki squeezed her eyes shut as the first tears started to fall, but it was no use. Her whole body shook as she lay on the beach, crying silently. When she finally calmed down a bit she noticed that the beach seemed oddly quiet. She raised one arm and peeked out from under it.

"Everyone has gone, Miss," said Athena, who was sitting next to her on the sand. "We thought it best to let you have some time to yourself. Fuzz is leading them to my mother's house in ImpHaven. She has a large house, so there should be room for everyone."

Nikki sat up and wiped her eyes. "Sorry about the crying. I'm just a bit stressed out."

Athena reached out a tiny hand and patted her on the shoulder. "You cry as much as you want Miss." She looked at Nikki with pity in her eyes. "Do you want to go home, Miss? Because if you do Fuzz and

I will escort you back to the portal at Castle Cogent this very day. You have been a great help to us, but we will not keep you here if you do not wish to stay."

"No," said Nikki. "Well, to be honest, yes. I do want to go home. But I can't. Not yet. I want to stay here and help, if I can. Help fight Rufius, and especially help the imps. I don't know how much help I can be, really, but I want to keep trying."

Athena stood up and put her arms around Nikki's shoulders, giving her a tight hug. "Thank you, Miss. You are very brave to choose to stay in a foreign land and help people who are strangers. We are very grateful. And you have helped already, many times."

Nikki took a deep breath and got to her feet. "Well, let's get on with it then. Lead the way."

Athena nodded and started climbing the sand dunes which lined the beach. At the top a path wandered through the sea grass toward ImpHaven. It was hard work trudging through the rolling sand dunes, and the bright sun made Nikki wish that sunglasses had already been invented in the Realm. After half an hour of walking they came to one of the breakwaters which guarded ImpHaven harbor.

Athena walked a few yards out onto the breakwater and stopped to take in the view. At their feet green waves crashed against huge boulders covered with barnacles. Spray from the ocean waves misted their backs but inside the harbor the water was still. Steep hills surrounded the harbor on three sides. Winding cobblestoned streets twisted across the hills and led down to a small beach at the far side of the harbor. White-washed cottages with thatched roofs and roses climbing up their walls clung to the hillsides. Fishing boats painted yellow and blue bobbed in the water and tall-masted ships unloaded cargo at long wooden piers. The harbor was smaller than the one at Kingston but it looked busy and prosperous.

"It is a lovely city, isn't it Miss?" said Athena.

"Beautiful," said Nikki. "Is this the only imp city?"

"The only large one," said Athena. "There are a few small villages, but most imps prefer to live here in ImpHaven. Over the centuries our country has been slowly gobbled up by the Realm. It used to be much larger, but every year we lose a bit more land. The big people take our farmland, put a fence around it, and declare it theirs. There is not much we can do about it. The King issued a proclamation a few years ago making these land-grabs illegal, but people have ignored it." She sighed. "The King is a friend to the imps, but he is not good at enforcing his own laws."

A piercing whistle suddenly sounded from across the harbor. Nikki could just make out a tiny figure waving at them from the steps of a large stone house.

"That is Fuzz," said Athena. "He is only calling to us because he does not like spending time with my mother."

"Is that her house?" asked Nikki.

"Yes," said Athena. "It is the largest house in ImpHaven. She inherited it from her own mother. That side of the family is quite wealthy, by imp standards. We imps don't have such grand palaces as Muddled Manor and Castle Cogent, but we do have what you might call our aristocracy. At least, my mother likes to think of herself as nobility. Fuzz teases her about it, which is one reason why she hits him with her cane. The other reason is because he deserves it."

She led Nikki back along the breakwater and down a cobbled road which followed the curve of the harbor. Imps were rushing back and forth with wheel barrows and handcarts, unloading the daily catch from the fishing boats.

"Is it lobster season?" asked Nikki, dodging a small red crustacean which was snapping at her feet with its over-sized claws. It scuttled under an over-turned wheelbarrow and a stray dog began barking furiously at it.

"Those are crayfish, Miss," said Athena. "The season for them is just ending. My mother's cook makes a wonderful crayfish stew.

Hopefully you will get to try some."

"Okay," said Nikki without much enthusiasm. Seafood had never been her favorite thing to eat. Fish and chips she could manage, but she'd always found the icky-looking stuff like crabs and lobsters hard to force down. A nice bowl of Mac and Cheese just seemed much more appealing than a plateful of claws and shells.

When they reached the far side of the harbor the road began to climb steeply. It zigzagged back and forth across the hillside in sharp hairpin curves. Down by the water they'd dodged wagons loaded with barrels of fish and baskets full of apples and potatoes. But up on the heights far above the harbor the road was quiet and empty. Blackberry bushes lined the road and the houses were spaced far apart. Each house had a flower garden full of dahlias, peonies, and roses.

"Here we are Miss," said Athena at last, stopping in front of the large stone house they'd see from across the harbor. "It is an impressive building, is it not?"

"Very grand," said Nikki. Most of the houses they'd passed had been one-story cottages with whitewashed walls and thatched roofs. This building was much more imposing. It was three stories tall and the walls were covered in gray stone. Tall columns rose from the entranceway all the way up to the roof. A long stone staircase bordered by blue hydrangea bushes led from the road up to the front door. A stone wall higher than Nikki's head ran along the property, enclosing a garden full of apple and peach trees. It reminded Nikki of a much smaller version of the Prince of Physics' huge estate in Kingston.

They started up the long stairs, but before they reached the top the front door of the house flew open with a bang.

"Finally!" said Fuzz, glaring down at them. "She nearly killed me this time!"

"I am sure you exaggerate," said Athena calmly. "You know very well she means no harm."

"No harm!" said Fuzz. "What do you call this?" He lifted up the hair covering his forehead to reveal a bright red lump the size of a duck egg. "That cane of hers should be declared a lethal weapon. I saw enough stars to make even the Sorcerer happy."

"Who's the Sorcerer?" asked Nikki.

"Just an imp who likes to watch the stars and planets," said Athena. "The people here call him the Sorcerer of the Stars because he goes up to the top of Foulweather Hill every night to watch the sky. He says the movement of the planets reveal great mysteries. Complete nonsense, of course. He has a few foolish followers who hang on his every word. He will say something silly, such as you must have a wedding only when Saturn is low on the horizon, and his followers will do exactly that. But he is harmless and an old friend of my mother. They were at school together. You will probably meet him. He likes to visit my mother because her cook is the best in ImpHaven."

"Yeah, he's here now," said Fuzz. "The little star-watching sponger."

"Fuzz!" said Athena. "That is no way to talk about one of your elders and one of ImpHaven's leading citizens."

Fuzz snorted. "If the Sorcerer is a leading citizen then the imps are in more trouble than I thought. He's a sponger through and through and that's all he'll ever be. And I should know, being an expert in the sponging profession myself. Your mother's put him in the best guest room and he's been there for two weeks now. He says he can't sleep in his own house because the North Star is aligned with his chimney and is sending bad luck down it. He's eating everything in your mother's pantry and he's probably drunk all of her ale."

"Let us hope so," said Athena severely. "That will mean less ale for you to guzzle."

Fuzz shrugged. "I'll just have to make do with what they serve at the Black Boar. Cheap, watered-down stuff, but better than nothing.

Maybe I'll just trot down there and have a pint or two."

Athena grabbed him by the collar as he tried to pass her. "You'll do nothing of the sort, Fuzz," she said, ignoring the strangled noise he was making. "It's nearly dinner time and my mother will expect you to dine with the rest of the company."

"Have a heart," said Fuzz, dodging away from her and rubbing his neck. "She's setting up a formal banquet in there. The good china is out and she's borrowed tables from the neighbors. There'll be at least fifty people sitting down to dinner. If your mother's cane doesn't kill me the small talk will."

"Making polite conversation will not kill you," said Athena, prodding Fuzz up the stairs and through the front door. "But my mother might if you do not appear for dinner. Now go and wash yourself. You smell like fish."

"Said the tuna to the mackerel," Fuzz muttered under his breath.

Nikki giggled, but then sniffed the sleeve of her tunic and realized he was right. They all smelled like the codfish which had been stored in the hold of Griff's ship. "Athena, maybe I should wash up too."

Athena patted her hand. "Yes, Miss. My mother has a lovely stone bath house out in the garden. We will have a nice long soak and find some clean clothes. Now, watch your . . ."

"Ouch!" Nikki rubbed the top of her head, which had banged against the lintel of the front door.

"Oh dear," said Athena. "I am sorry Miss. I should have warned you sooner. You will find all the doorways a bit low in this house. It was built for those of imp-size."

"It's okay," said Nikki a bit grumpily. Her nerves were still frayed from wrestling with Griff's ship and now she had a throbbing head to boot.

As they stepped into the entrance hall Nikki tried to get a look at the grand house, but it was difficult. Scores of imps were rushing around them carrying tablecloths, dinner plates, centerpieces of white roses, bread baskets, and spare chairs. Athena hustled her down a long hallway and out a side door where they joined Gwen and Linnea having a soak in the bath house. After lounging in the steamy water until her fingertips looked like prunes Nikki felt much better and ready to face the intimidating prospect of a large dinner party.

Chapter Two

Battle Plans

NIKKI DUCKED UNDER the tablecloth and quickly squeezed a bit more water out of her tunic. A small dribble of water ran down her chair and along the floor. The only spare clothes in the house were imp-sized, so Nikki, Gwen, Linnea, and Darius were all sitting around the dinner table in the same clothes they'd arrived in. They'd hastily washed their clothes in the bath house to get the fish smell out, but there'd been no time before dinner to dry them. Little puddles below their four chairs were forming underneath the main table, but no one seemed to care. They were wet but at least they weren't cold. A fire in the huge marble fireplace was giving off so much heat that Nikki could see steam rising off of Darius's leather vest.

Linnea, who was seated next to Nikki, was wiping sweat off of her face with a linen napkin while Rosie the mouse ran up and down her arm. "Rosamund, do stop running around like a wild thing and behave yourself." Linnea plucked Rosie off her arm and put her on the snowy white tablecloth. A few of the imps sitting near them looked askance at a mouse on the table, but Linnea didn't seem to notice. She picked out a dinner roll from the bread basket and broke off a piece, offering it to Rosie. Rosie snatched it up with her tiny paws and tucked it in her cheek, glaring with her beady eyes at the imp across from her. The imp quickly looked away and busied himself with the cream of potato soup he was eating.

Nikki was glad she'd left Cation locked in a bedroom upstairs. The spectacle of Cation pouncing on Rosie and eating her would definitely ruin more than a few appetites.

"Miss," said Athena, who was seated next to Nikki on her other side, "look what I have found in my mother's drawing room. A brand new batch of parchment. And a new pot of ink and freshly-cut quills. I will be able to write down your logical fallacies and your explanations and hypotheses again." She eagerly waved a feathered quill in the air, startling Rosie. The mouse scampered back up Linnea's sleeve and hid in her hair.

Nikki winced. Athena's habit of writing down everything she said was extremely embarrassing. It was enough to make her want to stop talking entirely. She was glad when a loud rapping sound suddenly rang through the room, causing an abrupt silence.

"Friends, neighbors, and esteemed guests, may I have your attention!" barked Athena's mother from her place at the head of the main table. She rapped loudly on the polished oak table with her cane, her grey ringlets shaking from the effort. "I have gathered you all here not only to welcome home my daughter and her companions, but also to begin a discussion which is long overdue. Namely, what to do about the deportation of the imps from the Realm of Reason. As I am sure you are all aware, imps have been flooding over our borders for many months now. Driven out of the Realm by pretenders to the throne. The King of the Realm has dropped the reins of control and is being overridden by these pretenders. The situation has become dire. Now, I will open the discussion to suggestions. Athena, present your ideas."

Nikki's eyes widened at such an abrupt order to speak in front of such a large group of people. She felt her face flush even though she wasn't the target of the order to speak.

Fortunately, Athena seemed to have no fear of addressing the crowded dining room. She cleared her throat and spoke in a firm voice. "My suggested plan of action is two-fold. First, we should continue to welcome any imp who requests sanctuary in ImpHaven. It is true that the city is becoming crowded, but there is plenty of room in the countryside. Second, we should keep open our lines of communication with the big people in the Realm who are friendly toward the imps. Most importantly, we should keep in touch with the King and the Prince of Physics. These are two of our most vital allies. Even if every imp in the Realm were to leave and crowd into ImpHaven we would still need the help of the King and the Prince. As we are all painfully aware, we are not capable of defending our land from incursions by the big people. If we resist they will send the Knights of the Iron Fist across our border to subdue us."

Gwen, who was sitting across from Nikki, cleared her throat and pushed back a lock of her pale blond hair which was dripping on the tablecloth. "I'm sorry to interrupt, but I've had an idea. May I speak?"

"Of course," said Athena, folding her hands on the tablecloth and nodding politely at Gwen.

Gwen's pale face turned pink from embarrassment, but she spoke firmly and clearly. "Water cannons," she said.

"Oh!" gasped Nikki. "Yes, that could work! But could you create enough pressure?"

Gwen smiled at her. "Yes, I believe so. I have a fair amount of experience with pumps. We would need to fashion one with a very large reservoir for the water as well as a large compressed air chamber. And we would need a power source. A hand-operated piston-type pump wouldn't create enough pressure. Maybe we could use a waterwheel as the power source. I'll draw up a design." She turned to Athena. "I'm not quite sure of the geography, but I believe the current border between the Realm and ImpHaven is the Roaring River?"

Athena nodded. "Yes, Miss. Our border used to extend many

miles past the river, but we have lost all the territory on the other bank."

"Good," said Gwen. "Well, I don't mean it's good that you have lost so much land, but it's good for our purposes. The Knights of the Iron Fist usually attack as a group. They seem either too lazy or too cowardly to spread out their forces and attack from many points all at once. So if they do invade ImpHaven, which seems more and more likely since they've joined forces with Rufius, then they will cross your border at only one point. I propose that we set up water cannons at the places where they will be most likely to cross the Roaring River."

"There's only two places where you can cross the river," Fuzz interjected. "The old stone bridge not far from here, and the ford where the river comes down from the Southern Mountains. The Roaring River is a very fast-flowing river. The current is so strong that not many people attempt to use the ford. You have to be roped together, which would be very dangerous for an iron-clad knight. If they slipped they'd sink straight to the bottom. Even on horseback it's difficult to cross at the ford."

Gwen nodded. "Then the bridge it is."

"And just what exactly is a water cannon, young lady?" demanded Athena's mother.

"It's a device which ejects a very powerful jet of water," said Gwen. "Powerful enough to knock an iron-clad knight clear off his horse."

Several of the imps at the main table started whispering among themselves.

"Quiet!" shouted Athena's mother, banging her cane on the table.

Silence descended immediately.

Nikki suppressed the urge to giggle. She knew a few teachers at her high school in Wisconsin who'd give anything to be able to make people be quiet the way Athena's mother could.

"Very well, young lady," said Athena's mother. "You will begin construction of this device at once."

Gwen looked a little startled at such an abrupt order, but she nodded politely.

"Wait just a darn minute!" A clanging sound came from the other end of the table as Athena's Aunt Gertie banged her knife and fork together. The elderly imp looked fully recovered from her stay in the dungeons of the Southern Castle. In contrast to Athena and Athena's mother, who were wearing plain gray woolen dresses, Aunt Gertie wore a frilly pink dress and had a jeweled tiara stuck in her grey hair. She looked rather like a five-year-old girl pretending to be a queen. "Just how do we know this contraption will work?" demanded Aunt Gertie. "What if it only knocks half the knights off their horses? What if it falls apart? What if we build this device at the bridge and they try to cross at the ford despite its dangers?"

"The Perfection Fallacy," muttered Nikki to herself.

"What was that, young lady?" asked Athena's mother, rapping her cane on the table again. "Speak up!"

Nikki turned bright red. She hadn't meant anyone to hear her, but Athena was giving her an encouraging pat on the arm and everyone else was looking at her. "I just meant that we should try Gwen's idea," she said, "We shouldn't refuse to try something just because it's not perfect. Nothing is ever perfect, but some things are worth doing anyway." Nikki abruptly stopped speaking, painfully aware that Athena was scribbling furiously with her quill on a piece of parchment.

"See, Miss?" said Athena when she had finished writing. "I have written down all of your fallacies again. At least the ones I remember. I might be missing one or two. I have the Post Hoc Fallacy, Counting the Hits, False Dilemma, the Appeal to Authority, the Appeal to Popularity, Straw Man, and Ad Hominem. And now I have added the Perfection Fallacy."

Athena's mother sighed loudly. "Put that parchment away. This no time for your scribblings. We have a battle to plan!"

Darius laughed, startling the imps on either side of him, who were only a third his size. "A battle? Surely you jest. A few defenses, certainly. That is a sensible plan. Place lookouts on your border. Build this water cannon which Gwen speaks of. But a battle? That is nonsense. There is no possible way imps can defeat the Knights of the Iron Fist in battle, no matter how lazy the knights are. In my opinion even a defense of your borders is foolish. You will be overrun in a few hours. A day at most. Your best option if Rufius orders the Knight to attack ImpHaven is to gather all your people and head south. Find a place far from the Realm and create a new homeland for yourselves."

Dead silence descended on the room. All of the imps stared at Darius in shock and horror.

Finally Athena's mother spoke. "Young man, the imps have been in the Realm for many, many centuries. We have been here as long as the big people. We will not be driven out of our lands. Not while there are any of us left to fight."

Darius shrugged his broad shoulders. "Well, then you will die."

Gwen gasped. "Darius!"

Darius looked at her unapologetically. "I'm sorry if I've offended anyone. But I speak only the truth. The imps cannot stand against the Knights. Or against the soldiers of the Realm, if Rufius gains control of them as well."

Gwen looked troubled but said nothing.

Nikki stared down at her plate. She hated to admit it, even to herself, but she thought Darius was right.

Linnea suddenly cleared her throat, startling everyone. The healer had been quietly feeding Rosie crumbs of bread and hadn't participated in the conversations during dinner. "Darius is correct," she said. Cries of anger came from all sides. Linnea calmly held up her hand until there was silence again. "He is correct that the imps have no hope of defending their lands if it comes to a battle. But there are other ways of defending your homeland. Allies. That is what will save you. And while you might feel under siege right now, you have more allies than you may think. The Prince of Physics, for one. He still holds great power in Kingston and in the surrounding lands along the sea coast. He has always been a friend to the imps. And in my own small village there are many people who work side by side with the few imps who still live nearby. There are many thousands of ordinary people throughout the Realm who do not hate the imps but instead think of them as friends and neighbors. If we could rally enough of them to support the imps I think we might stand a chance against Rufius and his knights."

"There is also the King," said Athena, banging her tiny fist on the table. "He has always been a friend to the imps, as was his father before him. He will help the imps stand up to this black-hearted Rufius and his gangs of thugs."

Nikki and Gwen exchanged a look. Nikki knew exactly what Gwen was thinking. They both thought that Athena's trust in the King was misplaced. The King was a weak man who was incapable of standing up to the tyrant Rufius was rapidly becoming.

Fuzz snorted. "The King spends all his time lounging in his rose garden in Castle Cogent. He won't stand up to Rufius. He's handed the reins of the Realm over to Rufius and Maleficious."

Nikki gasped, staring at Fuzz. "So you don't know," she said.

"Know what, Miss?" asked Athena.

"Maleficious is dead," said Nikki.

Gasps came from all over the room. Every head turned toward her.

"He's been dead for months," said Nikki. "I thought everyone knew. How could such an important piece of news be kept so quiet?"

"Easy," said Fuzz. "Maleficious is rarely seen by the public. He spends all his time skulking in Castle Cogent or in the Southern Castle in Kingston. He thinks mixing with ordinary people is beneath him.

How did you find out he was dead?" he asked Nikki.

"I found out when I was in Deceptionville," said Nikki. "You know, when I was dragged away while we were all sleeping in that blackberry patch. I was taken to Deceptionville. Anyway, Geber told me that Maleficious was dead. Geber is . . ."

Fuzz waved an impatient hand at her. "We know who Geber is," he said. "Everyone in the Realm knows. When he was younger he was a talented alchemist. He did some good work for the citizens of the Realm, especially in identifying harmful substances like mercury and lead. Before Geber lots of alchemists used to handle mercury with their bare hands. Lots of them went crazy. Anyway, these days Geber's just an old coot who's fond of issuing proclamations and declaring himself Deceptionville's Official Alchemist. He doesn't have any real power anymore, but he does have a lot of connections at Deceptionville's City Hall. That's probably how he found out about Maleficious's death."

Fuzz paused for a minute, frowning down at the tablecloth. "I'm trying to decide if this news is a good thing or a bad thing. What do you think, Athena old girl?"

Athena sniffed at being called an "old girl", but responded anyway. "I think it is good news," she said. "Rufius is very young. He does not have either the experience or the connections that Maleficious had. And he has not yet consolidated his grasp on power. I think we have been too passive. We should act now while there is still time."

Both Aunt Gertie and Athena's mother banged their canes on the table. "Well said," shouted Aunt Gertie. "Let's give 'em hell."

Chapter Three

The Sorcerer

"WHAT EXACTLY AM I supposed to be seeing?" Nikki whispered to Athena.

"Just stars, Miss," Athena replied. "All the portents and patterns which the Sorcerer claims to see in the sky exist only in his imagination. ImpHaven has decided it is the charming eccentricity of an elderly imp, but if you do not find it charming you are free to ignore him."

"Okay," whispered Nikki, dropping her gaze back down to earth and rubbing her sore neck. They had been standing in the rain on top of Foulweather Hill for more than an hour, gazing up at the stars. It wasn't the best night for stargazing. The Sorcerer would point out a constellation and then the rain clouds would blow across the sky and cover it. The elderly imp's followers were clustered around him, cheering whatever he said, but Nikki was sick of listening to him. She was even wetter than she'd been at tonight's dinner party and all she wanted was a hot bath and a good night's sleep.

She stared grumpily at the Sorcerer. He was not an imposing sight. He had scraggly grey hair and wore a midnight-blue robe spangled with silver stars and splotched with gravy stains. She wondered how such an unimpressive person had managed to collect so many followers. There'd been at least ten of them at the dinner party, and they'd all insisted she come up here to listen to the wondrous pronouncements of their leader. So far she hadn't heard anything the least bit wondrous. She strongly suspected that it wasn't any talent for preaching on the part of the Sorcerer which enthralled his followers. It was just that he was telling them what they wanted to hear. So far he'd told one imp that she was going to inherit a chest full of gold because it was her birthday and the planet Mercury was in retrograde. And an elderly imp had been informed that the young girl he was courting would fall madly in love with him due to the alignment of Saturn with the moon. Nikki knew that the retrograde motion of Mercury was a real phenomenon, where the planet appeared to go backwards in its orbit around the sun. But it was just an optical illusion, and what it had to do with chests full of gold totally escaped her. To Nikki the Sorcerer's prattling sounded a lot like Fortuna when she'd told fortunes in front of her giant fish tank back on the Isle of Ignorance. So Nikki was startled when the Sorcerer suddenly switched from chests full of gold to doom and gloom. Apparently the positions of Saturn and Venus now predicted that the all the imps would meet their doom on the banks of the Roaring River in a great battle with the Knights of the Iron Fist.

"Not an imp shall be left standing," intoned the Sorcerer in a raspy voice that sounded like dry sand on bare rock. "Blood will turn the river red and all of ImpHaven shall be emptied."

Athena sighed and sat down on a nearby bench which overlooked the dark streets of the town. Far below drunken cries from the pubs along the harbor floated up to them.

Nikki joined her on the bench.

"Just ignore him, Miss," said Athena. "Doom is his specialty. He loves predicting everyone's slaughter. Of course, he himself has never slaughtered so much as a sheep. He confines himself to imaginary bloodshed."

"Yeah, I know the type," said Nikki. "There are lots of boys in my school back home who love to play really violent video games, but if they were ever in a real war I think they'd just wet their pants and run away."

"What are video games, Miss?" asked Athena.

"Never mind," said Nikki. She gazed down at the town of ImpHaven. "This is quite a view. How far can we see from this hill? Can we see all the way to the border with the Realm?"

"Yes, Miss," said Athena. She turned away from the sea and pointed at a line of dark pine trees which were just visible on the horizon. "Those trees mark the border. The Roaring River flows just below them. Foulweather Hill is the tallest spot in ImpHaven until you reach the Southern Mountains. From here you can see all the way to Kingston on a clear day."

"It's too bad that Kira isn't here," said Nikki. "Her telescope would come in handy. We could station a spotter up here to keep a lookout. With a telescope they could spot the Knights of the Iron Fist from miles away. It would give us an advance warning of any invasion."

"What is a telescope, Miss?" asked Athena.

"It's a device for seeing long distances," said Nikki. "Kira had one on Griff's ship. I think hers was made by the Prince of Physics, but we might be able to make one ourselves, especially with Gwen's help. I know a little bit about the technology involved. It's a combination of lenses and mirrors, depending on what type of telescope you want to make."

Since telescopes already existed in the Realm Nikki didn't feel she was letting any modern secrets loose. Of course, her world had much more advanced telescopes than the Realm, but it wasn't like she had the technical specifications of the Hubble Space Telescope stored in her memory. At most she might be able to help Gwen re-create Galileo's crude refracting telescope, made around 1600 AD. She was pretty sure she could remember the details. They'd studied the design in her AP Physics class. It had two lenses. One was a convergent objective lens which was convex and caused the incoming light rays to converge to a point, and the other was a divergent eyepiece lens which was concave and made the light rays parallel again before they hit your eye. The lenses would be a bit tricky to grind, but Gwen had experience with that. Once the lenses were made you just stuck them into a long wooden tube at the correct angles.

"Notice how Mercury is crossing the constellation of the Long-Necked Swan!" the Sorcerer suddenly shouted, gesturing excitedly at the sky. "This has ever been a portent of death and destruction!"

Both Athena and Nikki sighed.

"Astrology?" said Nikki. "Really? I thought you said the people of the Realm didn't believe in it. When we were on the Isle of Ignorance it was Fish Fortunes they were all so excited about. Quite a lot of people there were caught up in Fortuna's Fish Fortunes scam."

Athena shrugged. "There are a lot of silly superstitions in the Realm, Miss. Each town seems to have its own. I don't believe Fish Fortunes ever spread past the Isle of Ignorance, despite Fortuna's efforts. The belief that the stars control our destiny is only popular among a small group of imps here in ImpHaven, mainly due to the Sorcerer and his endless pontificating. It never caught on among the big people in the Realm. In the large cities like Kingston and Deceptionville there are many little superstitions based on gambling games such as dice and dart throwing. Spitting over your left shoulder is a common practice before throwing your dice or dart. Not a pleasant custom for anyone standing behind you. In the countryside among the farmers they have customs that involve cutting fruit. They slice an apple in half and count the seeds. An odd number of seeds means a pregnant woman will have a baby boy, even means a baby girl. Or they cut a pomegranate to predict how their crops will do. An even number of pomegranate seeds means you will have a good harvest in the fall. These various superstitions are strange behaviors which I have never entirely understood. As far as I can make out it has to do with trying to exert control over your life or your surroundings. Personally I think they are a waste of time. I prefer more direct methods. If you want a good harvest you should work hard, till your soil, sow your seeds, and scare off any birds who try to eat your ripening grain. Sitting around cutting open pomegranates is pointless."

Nikki nodded. "Yes, superstition is a waste of time, but a lot of people seem to get some kind of emotional kick from it. I mean, they must be getting something out of it or they wouldn't do it. Astrology has survived in my world for thousands of years. I think the appeal of astrology has a bit to do with the grandeur of the stars. People look up at the night sky and they're awestruck at the immensity. They think there must be powerful forces up there controlling the universe. I've also noticed that people who feel powerless down on earth tend to be more superstitious than wealthy and powerful people. I can kind of understand why. If you're poor and powerless superstition is all you've got."

"Possibly," said Athena. "Though not all of the Sorcerer's followers are poor. That imp over there in the purple velvet cloak is one of the richest citizens in ImpHaven. He is currently spending a large amount of gold to build the Sorcerer a mansion on the same street as my mother's house. I personally have mixed feelings about this. The gold could be put to better use helping our poorer citizens, but on the other hand at least this new mansion will get the Sorcerer out of my mother's guest bedroom."

Nikki chuckled. "He does seem to have a scammer's knack for sponging off people." She looked out to sea. Moonlight was shining down on the waves through gaps in the clouds. She could just make out the dark masts of Griff's ship down on the beach. Fortunately the ship had drifted up onto the sand. It didn't look in any danger of being carried out to sea. Griff would probably forgive them for borrowing her ship, but she wouldn't be too happy if it sank.

Nikki frowned suddenly. A dark blob was plowing through the waves not far from Griff's ship, heading toward ImpHaven. "Do you see that?" she asked.

Athena looked where she was pointing. "I do, Miss. It looks like a fishing boat, though they do not generally do any night fishing around here." She stood up. "Come, Miss. We should report this to the ImpHaven Watch and to the Harbormaster. We don't often get strange boats along this part of the coast, and in these uncertain times it is better to be cautious."

Nikki followed Athena down the long flight of stone steps which wound around the hill. Behind them she could hear the Sorcerer still holding forth on the constellations. No one seemed to notice they'd left.

The stone steps were slippery from the rain and Nikki was too busy paying attention to her feet to notice where they were going. As they wound around and around the hill all she could see was the wet grass bordering the steps and the rivulets of rain water which occasionally crossed her path. When she finally looked up she was surprised to find they were already at the harbor. Looking back she could see the candlelight in the windows of the houses twinkling far above her.

"I used a shortcut, Miss," said Athena. "Foulweather Hill has been a lookout for centuries and it is useful to have a quick route from the hill to the harbor. Come. That building over there with the two oars crossed above the door houses both the Watch and the Harbormaster."

Athena led the way along the wooden boardwalk which circled the harbor.

Nikki wrinkled her nose at the strong smell of fish. Stray dogs were sniffing for scraps along the wet boardwalk.

Athena climbed the front steps of the Harbormaster building and pushed through a creaky door. They entered a dusty hall with crude pictures of boats painted on the walls. Piles of rusted lobster traps and coils of moldy ropes lurked in the dark corners.

Nikki sneezed from all the dust.

"Who's there?" shouted a voice from somewhere above their heads.

They waited as footsteps clomped along the ceiling above them and stomped down the rickety staircase which led to the hall.

"Oh, it's you Athena." An imp wearing a heavy raincoat and muddy boots strode up to them.

Nikki was surprised by how young he was. She'd been expecting a grizzled old seadog. Instead he looked not much older than twenty and was taller than most of the imps she'd met.

"Miss, this is our Harbormaster and a member of the Watch," said Athena. "Triton, allow me to introduce Nikki. She is a King's Emissary."

"Goodness me," said Triton, shaking Nikki's hand with a twinkle in his eye. "I thought only Athena held that eminent title."

Athena brushed this aside with an impatient wave of her hand. "There is a ship nearing ImpHaven. It is almost to the harbor entrance. It was hard to tell in the dark, but I do not think it is one of our fishing fleet."

Triton frowned. "Just one ship? How long ago did you see it?"

"Just the one," said Athena. "We spotted it from Foulweather Hill ten minutes ago."

"All our ships are in port," said Triton, heading for the front door. "It's not one of ours. It could be a merchant ship from Kingston, but they usually send us word by carrier pigeon before their arrival. We'd better have a look."

They followed Triton out into the rainy night and along the boardwalk. He headed at a fast pace toward the breakwater at the mouth of the harbor. They passed dark warehouses which were closed for the night. Patches of candlelight shone in the windows of the many pubs lining the harbor. The night was quiet except for the occasional drunken shout from a pub and the creak of the wooden hulls of the fishing fleet rubbing against their moorings. They arrived at the breakwater just in time to see the dark hull of a ship sail into port. It wasn't a huge three-master like Griff's ship, but it was big enough to loom over them in the darkness like a monster from the depths of the sea. It came toward them under full sail, then its speed dropped as its billowing sails collapsed and were secured to the masts by dark figures. The ship drifted up to the nearest open dock and came to a halt, its hull grinding against the wooden pier.

A rope ladder was flung over the side and a tall, athletic figure climbed gracefully down and lashed the bow of the ship to the pier with a thick rope.

"Krill!" exclaimed Nikki.

"Hello there," said Krill as he rushed past them to the stern of the ship. He fastened it to the pier with another rope. "Didn't take us much time to catch up to you, did it? Griff'll follow ship thieves to the ends of the earth, you know."

"Um, about that," said Nikki.

Krill grinned. "Just kidding. We spotted our ship on the beach as we came down the coast. We dropped off a few of the crew to check for damages. The rudder's a bit banged up, but otherwise everything seems ship-shape. Griff was more worried about you than the ship. Kira too. And that little nutter Curio was beside himself. He kept insisting he was going to run off on his own and challenge all the Knights of the Iron Fist to hand-to-hand combat. Griff had to lock him in a closet at the Prince's house until we could arrange for another ship. We all thought you'd been kidnapped."

Nikki was glad it was dark. She could feel her face turning red with embarrassment. "No, I just climbed the wall of the Prince's estate and went up to the Southern Castle. I was worried about my friends. I met them outside the castle walls and well, it's a long story, but basically we escaped from Kingston by stealing your ship. I'm sorry if you were worried about me. I'm fine. This is my friend Athena, and this is Triton, the Harbormaster here at ImpHaven."

Krill nodded politely. "Any chance of a hot meal and a bed? Most of the crew will be staying onboard, but a few of us would like to get our land legs."

"Of course," said Triton. "The Black Boar has rooms for big people, and they make a very tasty chicken pie. It's just over there, past the lobster traps."

"Wonderful," said Krill. "If you'll just wait here a second I'll tell them."

He clambered up the rope ladder and disappeared over the railing of the ship.

A few minutes later Krill, Kira, Griff, Curio, and the imp Tarn climbed down the ladder.

"Nikki!" shouted Kira, running up to give her a hug. "You gave us such a scare!"

"Hello, Miss!" said Curio. He hopped up and down excitedly. "Here you are all safe and sound. I knew you would be, of course. I knew those knights could never catch you. But if they ever do don't you worry. I'll make 'em pay. I'll give 'em a rat-tat-tat on those tin cans they call helmets until they see double. They'll fall right off their horses. They'll stumble around like drunks after the pubs close and they'll fall right into the nearest river. And if they don't fall in I'll push 'em in." He put his hand to his right side and unsheathed what looked like a very short sword.

Nikki gasped, rounding on Kira and Griff. "You didn't! A sword! Are you nuts?"

Griff laughed. "Don't worry. It's wooden. I had Krill carve it for him. It keeps him busy. We tied an old pillow to one of the masts and he slashed at it all the way down the coast."

Tarn the imp gave a loud snort. "The little piker's been driving me crazy with all his running up and down the deck, up to the crows nest, down into the hold. Wouldn't sit still for a minute. Couldn't mend me nets it was so annoying. Like a cloud of wasps buzzing round me head it was."

Curio laughed and hopped around making a buzzing noise between his missing front teeth. "Are we off to fight the knights, Miss? I bet I can take on twenty all by myself. They're cowards, they are. Anybody who covers himself in metal is a coward. And they're always sticking their long swords in people's faces. I saw one in Kingston stick his sword right into the face of an old lady who weren't doing nothing. She was just walking down the street carrying a basket of apples. This knight, this pile of poop stuffed into a tin can, sticks his sword right in her face and yells at her to get out of his way. I'll show you what we should do to worthless cowards like that." He darted up to a pile of lobster traps and started hacking at them with his wooden sword.

Krill sighed. "It's a pile of work keeping the little nutter out of trouble, let me tell you." He grinned at Nikki. "Griff assigned me to watch him, but I officially turn the task over to you."

"Thanks," sighed Nikki, watching Curio trying to pull his sword out of the tangle of lobster traps.

"Miss," said Athena. "Perhaps you should introduce us."

"Oh, right," said Nikki. "Sorry. This is my friend Kira, the ship's navigator and first-mate. The brave soldier with the sword is Curio. And this is Griff, the captain of the ship we, um, borrowed."

Griff gave Nikki a bit of a look. It implied that ship-borrowing would only be allowed once. She politely shook hands with Athena and Triton. "I met the Harbormaster last year when we docked here to fix one of our sails, but I don't believe I've ever met the King's Emissary."

Athena gave her a startled look. "You know who I am, Miss?"

Griff nodded. "Seen your wanted poster, I have. On every wall in

Kingston. Usually next to a picture of an imp with a stylish goatee."

"That's Fuzz," said Nikki. "He's also here in ImpHaven."

"Well," said Athena, "I would like to hear the news from Kingston, but there will be time for that later. Let us get inside out of this rain."

Athena and Triton led the way along the boardwalk to the Black Boar.

"Nobody bothered to introduce *me*," muttered Tarn, stumping along at the back of the group. "Typical."

Krill laughed and slapped the imp on the back, which produced around round of grumpy muttering.

"You should be comfortable here," said Triton as he led them up the front steps of the Black Boar and held open the heavy oak door. "They get sailors down from Kingston on occasion, so they're used to big people."

A shout went up as they stepped into the common room of the pub.

At first Nikki thought that their arrival had startled the customers, but she soon realized that the imps hadn't even noticed them. Some kind of dice game was going on in the middle of the room and a large crowd was placing bets and shouting at the players. Many of the imps were smoking pipes and the air was thick with smoke.

"Don't wait up for me," said Krill with a grin. He slid through the crowd and crouched down to watch the game.

"Just don't lose every coin you possess," called Griff.

Krill just waved an impatient hand, his attention fixed on the game.

"Nikki and me'll keep an eye on him," said Kira, linking her arm in Nikki's and pulling her over to the dice game.

"Um," said Nikki. "Shouldn't we see about getting some rooms?" She was cold and wet and just wanted to go to bed. Watching Krill play dice was not on the top of her list.

"Griff'll take care of the lodgings," said Kira. "Normally I'd just let Krill lose as much coin as he wants, but he happens to be holding some of mine. Whenever we're in port I give him some of my coin for safekeeping. He's harder to rob than I am, being so big. Not that I expect much trouble here in ImpHaven. It's a peaceful place. But there's always a few dodgy sailors in any port, even here."

They squeezed through the crowd until they found a spot just behind Krill.

"So, chaps," said Krill. "What are the rules? This game is new to me."

Nikki noticed a few eyes light up at this and guessed that they considered Krill an easy target.

A scruffy imp with a black beard held up the two dice he was about to roll. "Rules are simple. You wins one gold coin ifs you throws a two, three, four, five, nine, ten, eleven, twelve. You loses five gold coins ifs you throws a six or eight. You loses ten gold coins if you throws a seven." He grinned, showing black holes where most of his teeth should have been. "Lots of chances to win, sonny."

Krill nodded to show that he understood.

Nikki frowned, wondering if he really did. There were eight winning coins and only three losing ones, but she couldn't help noticing that the numbers most likely to come up, six, seven, and eight, were also the ones assigned losses. Losing ten gold coins on a seven was especially bad, as the number seven was the most likely number to come up when rolling two dice. It was standard probability. There were six possible combinations for seven: 2 and 5, 5 and 2, 3 and 4, 4 and 3, 6 and 1, 1 and 6. A total of six combinations out of the thirty-six possible outcomes of two dice. Six and eight weren't quite as bad, having five combinations each, but they still occurred more frequently than the other numbers. It seemed to her that the game was heavily in favor of the house, or whoever was running the game. Probably the imp with the black beard.

She tried to do a quick expected value calculation in her head, which would tell her just how much advantage the house had. The formula was percentage * value = expected value. For the number seven the percentage was 6\36, or 1\6, so the expected value for seven was (1\6) * (-10). About -1.67. Negative because you lost money when you rolled a seven. She calculated the expected value for each of the numbers two through twelve and then summed them all up. It was difficult without a calculator, but she did her best and came up with an expected value for the game of negative 2.44. A negative expected value for the whole game meant that the house made money and the gamblers lost money. They might get lucky in the short run, but if they played long enough they'd be guaranteed to lose money. In this case a *lot* of money.

"I'd get your money back *now*," she whispered to Kira. "Before he starts playing. The odds aren't in his favor."

Kira nodded. She thumped Krill on the back. "I want my coin back."

Krill shook his head, still watching the game. "Nah, hold your horses. I'll double your money right quick."

Kira thumped him harder. "Give it back. *Now*."

Krill sighed. He reached into his tunic and pulled out a small leather pouch. "Your loss," he said, tossing the pouch to Kira.

Kira snorted. "*Your* loss, more likely." She linked arms again with Nikki. "Come on, let's get some sleep. I'm not going to stay up all night watching another Krill catastrophe."

Chapter Four

Preparations

"I'M NOT STANDING up here on this soggy mound getting' me feet wet while the rest of you laze about in comfort guzzling all the ale in ImpHaven." Tarn spit into the wet grass on top of Foulweather Hill and glared up at Griff.

Griff sighed. "I've told you five times already, you bilious barnacle, you're not the only one assigned to lookout duty. Kira will take her turn in four hours, then Krill after her, then the rest of the crew." She handed Tarn the small telescope that Kira had retrieved from her quarters on their beached ship.

"Don't break that," warned Kira. "It's the only one I've got."

Tarn grumbled a reply and plopped down on the stone bench that Nikki and Athena had sat on the night before. He hopped up again immediately, swearing and wiping the seat of his pants, which were now soaking wet.

Nikki choked back a giggle. She felt a little guilty for laughing at him, but only a little. Tarn wasn't her favorite imp. Not by a long shot. It was more than just his grumpiness. When they were eating breakfast that morning at the Black Boar she'd caught him looking at her with a calculating expression, as if wondering how much she'd fetch at market. As if she was a prize pig or something. It had crossed her mind that he might try to sell information about her whereabouts to Rufius or the Knights of the Iron Fist. She tried to tell herself that Griff wouldn't have him on her crew if he was untrustworthy, but she couldn't shake her suspicion of him. She turned away from him and started down the stone steps which wound around the hill.

Kira caught up to her. "So, what's on the agenda for today?"

"Water cannons," said Nikki.

"What?" asked Kira, her long braids swinging as she walked. Today they had purple ribbons twined around them. "What the heck are water cannons?"

"You'll see," said Nikki. "I'll let Gwen explain them. She's a friend of mine who's a real expert at that kind of thing. She's drawing up a design. We're going to use them to defend ImpHaven against the Knights of the Iron Fist. If they invade, that is. Hopefully they won't, but it's better to be prepared."

Kira nodded solemnly. "It's not a good time to be an imp. I feel really bad for them. Being out at sea so much we miss a lot of what's happening in the Realm. I was shocked to find out how much had changed in Kingston recently. Rufius is very close to having all the soldiers stationed at the Southern Castle under his complete control. If he gets control of both the soldiers and the Knights of the Iron Fist then it's not just the imps who'll be in danger. He'll be able to mount a takeover of the entire Realm. I think I'd leave if that happened."

"Really?" asked Nikki. "You wouldn't stay and fight?"

Kira frowned, kicking a bit of gravel off the steps and watching it bounce down the hill. "We're pirates. Cod fishermen, when we're trying to be respectable. We go where the cod are. The ocean's big. Plenty of places to hide from Rufius and his thugs. We could sail to the Southern Isles. It's hot, with insects as big as your hand, but at least we'd be free. No knights ordering people around at swordpoint."

"Well I'm staying here to help the imps," said Nikki stubbornly. "If everyone runs away from bullies then the bullies just get nastier.

They realize people won't fight back."

Kira sighed. "The imps *can't* fight back. Well, they can try, but they won't succeed. It would be suicide. They're simply too small to defend themselves from armed knights on horseback."

"Size isn't the only thing that matters," said Nikki. "The imps have brains, and allies, and a working water cannon." She pointed at a gush of water which had suddenly arched into the sky over their heads. "Looks like Gwen got one built a lot faster than I expected." She headed toward the sound of people clapping and cheering.

"Nikki! Just in time!" Gwen waved at her from the grassy bank of a fast-moving stream. The stream ran through a field of yellow-flowered mustard plants at the bottom of Foulweather Hill. Athena and Darius were standing nearby. Fuzz was stretched out on the bank of the stream chewing lazily on a mustard stalk. Linnea was out at the edge of the field gathering the mustard plants. Curio was running across the field trying to catch a white butterfly which kept fluttering just out of his reach.

When Curio spotted Nikki he sprinted toward her. "Miss! Watch us blast the knight! C'mon, show her! Show her!" He jumped up and down and waved wildly at two imps on the far side of the stream.

The imps laughed and picked up a straw figure which was lying in the grass. They perched it on top of a wooden sawhorse that had a broom for a head and mustard stalks for a tail.

Darius lifted up a small wooden water gate near the edge of the stream. Water rushed through the gate and along a newly-dug trench into a wooden barrel sitting in a hole in the ground. A canvas hose was attached to the side of the barrel. After a moment a gush of water squirted out of the hose. Gwen picked it up and aimed it at the straw knight. The straw figure was knocked backwards off its sawhorse and flopped to the ground in soggy defeat.

Curio whooped and ran around in circles pumping his fists.

Gwen shook her head and pushed a lock of pale blond hair away from her face. "Celebration is premature, I'm afraid. There isn't enough pressure yet. Straw is a lot easier to knock over than a grown man in full armor."

"I thought you were going to use a water wheel as a power source," said Nikki.

"My original plan was to attach a rotating arm to the central hub of a waterwheel and use that to work a pump," said Gwen. "But it would have been a complicated design and liable to breakage. Then Fuzz took me over to the old stone bridge, which is the only way to cross the Roaring River, and I realized there was a much simpler solution." She pointed down at the trench which ran from the stream through the mustard field to the barrel full of water. "Even this small stream creates quite a bit of force when you suddenly divert some of its water into a narrow trench. The Roaring River is much larger than this stream and its current is much swifter. The river is on a steep downward slope as it arrives in ImpHaven from the Southern Mountains. By the time it flows under the old stone bridge it is rushing along at a furious pace. Just before it reaches the bridge it drops over a twenty-foot high waterfall which increases its speed even more. My new plan is to dig a trench similar to what we have here, running from just below the waterfall to the stone bridge. We'll build a water gate which can be opened very quickly, sending a rush of water along the trench and into a barrel which will feed our water cannon. Due to the speed of the Roaring River we should get more than enough force to knock a knight off his horse."

"Good old PE," said Nikki. "Potential energy."

Gwen raised a questioning eyebrow.

"The force created by the river's current is called potential energy," said Nikki. "PE is stored energy, usually caused by gravity, like when you drop a rock off a tall building. The taller the building the harder the rock will hit the ground. The formula is PE = MGH. M is mass, like the mass of a rock you drop off a building. G is gravity. And

H is the height of the building. For our water cannon M would be the mass of the water falling off the waterfall and H would be the height of the waterfall. When the water is ejected from the hose and hits the straw man it becomes kinetic energy. The energy stored by PE is kind of being used up. Potential energy gets converted to kinetic energy, the energy of motion."

"What's gravity?" asked Kira.

"It's what pulls objects toward the center of the earth," said Nikki. "It kind of acts like a force, though I don't think it actually is. My physics teacher explained it in school, but I didn't really understand it. He said it had to do with warped space around a massive object like the earth."

Both Kira and Gwen looked at her like she'd grown an ear in the center of her forehead. Nikki quickly decided that the warped space of General Relativity wasn't something she needed to introduce to the Realm. She didn't understand it anyway. It would have to wait until she got to college, if she ever got back home. Trying to explain it in the middle of a mustard field in the Realm of Reason was pointless.

"Never mind," she said. She walked over to the barrel and peered inside. Darius had closed the water gate again and the barrel was only half full of water. The hole where the hose was attached was visible and Nikki thought she could see how Gwen had designed it to increase the flow rate. It was smaller than the hole where the water entered the barrel from the trench. She picked up the hose and examined the wooden nozzle attached to the end of the canvas tube. The shape of the nozzle reminded her of a fire hose. There was a handle attached to what looked like a small suction pump. When she moved the handle back and forth she could feel air being pumped into the nozzle. She didn't know much about fluid dynamics, but it looked like the nozzle pumped air into the stream of water coming from the barrel. When the air was forced into the water it increased the pressure inside the nozzle, creating a stronger stream than just water alone. There was also a narrow section of the nozzle, like the Venturi in a water pump or carburetor, which forced the stream of water through a smaller diameter. That lowered the pressure but increased the flow rate.

Gwen came over to her. "I think this will work pretty well if we only have to defend the bridge against one knight at a time. But if the Knights of the Iron Fist get smart about an attack on ImpHaven they'll charge across the bridge in a large group, moving at a gallop. It's unlikely my water cannon would be able to stop them."

Nikki nodded, her shoulders slumping. They might be able to hold off the knights for a while, but any determined attack on ImpHaven would eventually succeed. She tried not to feel defeated even before any attack had been launched, but she couldn't help wondering if Darius was right. The only solution for the imps was to leave their homeland.

"There is another possibility," said Gwen. "Another method of defense which might work. Remember that explosion I demonstrated in the yard in front of my house in Deceptionville? Black powder. That's what I call the substance that I used. It has tremendous power. I used it to escape from the dungeons of the Southern Castle in Kingston, when Rufius had me imprisoned there. A relatively small quantity of it was enough to knock down a stone wall two feet thick. I believe it could also be used to propel a small projectile, such as a lump of lead. Perhaps using a modified crossbow. I'm not sure, I'd have to draw up a design. But if we could produce enough weapons which used this black powder I feel certain we could repel any attack."

Nikki's heart sank into her shoes. She clutched the side of the barrel for support.

"What's wrong?" asked Gwen in concern. "You've turned pale as a ghost."

Nikki just shook her head. She didn't know how to convey her horror of guns to someone who'd never seen one. How to convey their destructive power to someone from a land which only had to fear swords and arrows. She took a deep breath and let go of the barrel. There was no point in falling to pieces. She was trying to think of a way to talk Gwen out of using her black powder when a shout suddenly went up from the top of Foulweather Hill.

Nikki and Gwen looked up. Tarn was waving at them from the top of the hill. He pointed toward the harbor.

Everyone in the mustard field squinted up at Tarn, trying to figure out what he was saying, but Athena didn't hesitate. She raced to the bottom of the hill and started up the stone steps as fast as her short legs could carry her.

Nikki and Kira ran after her, soon catching up.

"Go!" gasped Athena. "Don't wait for me!"

Nikki nodded and raced up the winding stairs two at a time. By the time she reached the top she was so out of breath she could barely speak. "What is it?" she managed to gasp out.

In answer Tarn pointed at the mouth of the harbor.

Far below a black-sailed ship was passing the breakwaters. It slowed, dropping its sails, but it didn't dock. Instead the creak of an anchor chain echoed across the harbor and the ship dropped anchor and came to a halt right in the middle of the harbor. A figure up on the crows nest pulled at a rope and a banner unfurled from the top of the mast. It was solid black with a silver sword piercing a gold crown.

Kira stumbled up the last few steps and took the telescope from Tarn. She peered at the banner. "I don't recognize it," she gasped, trying to catch her breath. "It's not the King's flag, nor the flag of Kingston."

"May I look, Miss?" gasped Athena, appearing over the crest of the hill.

Kira handed her the telescope.

Athena stared through it for a long while, then lowered it, nodding grimly. "Yes, it is as I suspected. It is the traitor Rufius. He is there in the bow, skulking just behind the figurehead."

As they watched a dinghy was lowered over the side of the ship. Three men climbed down a rope ladder into the waiting dinghy. They rowed to the nearest dock, tying up to it while a group of fishermen who were cleaning their catch watched nervously.

The new arrivals ignored the fishermen and marched purposefully along the boardwalk to the headquarters of the Harbormaster.

Nikki heard a faint click from across the harbor as the front door of the building closed behind them. She glanced down at Athena. "I'll admit it doesn't look good, but it doesn't look like an invasion, exactly. It kind of looks like a diplomatic mission. Maybe they just want to start some kind of negotiation with the imps?"

Athena shook her head grimly. "No, Miss. I do not think so. I suspect they have come to insist on our surrender. They think we will give up without a fight."

Chapter Five

The Delegation

NIKKI COUGHED AS a cloud of dust rose around her. The creaky old oaken chair with its ancient red velvet seat looked like it hadn't been sat on in years. Little puffs of dust were rising all over the room as people took their seats around the huge polished table. An imp was still vigorously polishing one corner as the delegation from Kingston took their seats at the head of the table.

Over their heads faded banners dripping with cobwebs displayed the crests of ImpHaven's oldest fishing families. The cavernous meeting hall in the headquarters of the Harbormaster also displayed a large blue banner showing stone walls encircling a crude depiction of Foulweather Hill. Athena, who was seated next to Nikki, told her that this was the banner of ImpHaven's Watch. Nikki gathered that the Watch was a kind of informal police force. Triton, who sat at one end of the table alongside Fuzz and Athena's Aunt Gertie, was both the Harbormaster and the head of the Watch.

Nikki was the only non-imp at the table except for the delegation from Kingston. Athena had asked Gwen, Linnea, and Darius to wait at her mother's house. Griff and her crew were waiting at the Black Boar.

Nikki turned her head at a noise from behind her. Rufius was lounging in a chair against the wall, one leg draped over the armrest.

He winked at her as he cracked another walnut, dropping its shell on the floor. He was wearing his usual black tunic and sandals, both spotless, but Nikki noticed something new. He had a broach in the shape of a silver sword pinned to the shoulder of his tunic. It was the same symbol as the one on the banner flying from the mast of the ship he'd arrived in.

A loud banging suddenly echoed through the hall.

"All right, let's get this over with," barked Aunt Gertie, banging her cane on the table. She was still dressed in pink ruffles, with her sparkly tiara perched crookedly in her grey hair. Her dress sense didn't convey authority so much as childish silliness. And the three cushions she was sitting on didn't help. The delegates from Kingston didn't bother to hide their grins.

"What's yer hurry Granny?" asked one, a pudgy young blond man in a too-tight tunic. "We've got loads of time."

"You will address me as Magistrate, young man," said Aunt Gertie, her cane crashing down on the table. "I was presiding over disputes of law before your parents were even born."

Triton waved a calming hand. "Perhaps we should start by hearing what our visitors from Kingston have to say. If they could state the purpose of their visit it would be helpful. I think it is clear to all in this room that you are neither fishermen nor merchants wishing to trade with ImpHaven. To be blunt, why are you here?"

The oldest delegate, a hunched man with stringy grey locks down to his shoulders, cleared his throat. He pulled a piece of parchment from his tunic and read from it. "To all the citizens of ImpHaven, it has been decided that the southern-most province of the Realm, hereafter named Kingston Province, is in need of good farmland to feed its growing population. To that end we are here to open discussions with ImpHaven regarding a transfer of land to the province of Kingston." He folded the parchment and put it back in his tunic.

There was a long moment of silence in the room. Most of the imps around the table looked frightened, but sparks were practically shooting out of the eyes of Fuzz and Aunt Gertie. Triton looked wary. Athena stared down at the polished table top, still as a statue.

Triton cleared his throat. "As I'm sure you're aware, ImpHaven cannot afford to lose any more land. Farmers from the Realm have been illegally taking our land for years. They come in large numbers, fence the land, and forcibly remove any imps who were living there."

The grey-haired delegate shrugged. "Your disputes with the Realm's farmers are not our concern. Our mission is a royal one, approved by the King himself. The King wishes to extend the Realm's borders to the Southern Mountains."

A shout went up from the imps. Fists banged on the table.

"Extending the Realm all the way to the Southern Mountains would wipe ImpHaven off the map!" Triton exclaimed.

"Not at all," said the delegate. "We have no designs on your little city here by the harbor. The harbor is too small for many of our ships, and we already have a much larger port at Kingston."

"So you propose what, exactly?" asked Triton. "That all the imps across our lands cram themselves into the city?"

"Precisely," said the delegate, smirking. "I'm sure it shall be very cosy. I am also sure that you would not object to taking in the imps who currently reside in the Realm. They are longing to live once more in their homeland."

Aunt Gertie banged her cane on the table. "I presume you have a signed writ from the King regarding this outrage," she said. "We will not enter into any negotiations with nincompoops who have not one speck of authority."

A chuckle came from Rufius. "My good imp, I assure you I have all the authority required. I am the King's representative. I have taken over the position of chief advisor to his majesty. I was formally appointed to this position after the death of my patron, Maleficious."

Aunt Gertie snorted. "And what does the Prince of Physics have to say about all this nonsense, young man? Answer me that."

At the Prince's name the amused smirked temporarily slipped from Rufius's face. He closed his eyes for a second. When he opened them again hatred could be seen burning deep within them. "The Prince is not involved in this matter. He confines himself to his business matters in Kingston. He hardly leaves his estate nowadays."

Athena turned and looked him in the face. "That is because you have armed knights surrounding his grounds."

Rufius grinned at her. "What the Knights of the Iron Fist do is their own concern. They certainly don't take orders from me."

Athena was about to angrily contest this statement when the door of the hall suddenly crashed open.

Darius ran in, out of breath, his tool belt clanging.

Everyone stared at him as he held up a hand, trying to catch his breath.

"Knights!" he finally managed to gasp out. "The Knights of the Iron Fist have invaded ImpHaven!"

All the imps around the table gasped as color drained from their faces. They sat as though paralyzed.

Nikki was shocked too, but not so shocked that she lost her head. She noticed at once that neither Rufius nor the delegates seemed surprised by this news.

"So this was just a distraction," she said, turning to Rufius. "You kept us all here, wasting time, while your knights invaded without warning."

Rufius just smirked and cracked another walnut.

"We tried to hold them off," said Darius. "We built Gwen's water cannon on the bank of the Roaring River and we were just testing it when a troop of knights fifty strong suddenly came charging across the old stone bridge. They must have ridden up to the borders of ImpHaven during the night. The lookout on Foulweather Hill never spotted them. We pounded the front of the pack with the water cannon and managed to knock several off their horses, but the ones behind just jumped over their fallen comrades and charged on."

Athena was the first imp to overcome her shock. "Were any of the imps hurt?" she asked.

Darius shook his head. "No. The imps just ran. As did Gwen and myself. We had no choice. The knights were in full armor, with shields and broadswords. There was no way to defend against them."

The three delegates at the far end of the table pushed back their chairs and stood up. "Well," said the grey-haired delegate, "You can see how the matter stands. The knights have their instructions. They are even now spreading throughout the countryside of ImpHaven, rounding up the inhabitants and herding them into the city. I suggest you send messengers throughout your lands to caution your citizens against resistance. That will avoid any unnecessary bloodshed."

The pudgy blond delegate smacked his fist against his palm. "And we'll be taking you lot, you self-declared leaders of the imps, back to our ship. We have some nice comfy cells in our hold, with good strong locks." He made a grab for the imp sitting nearest him.

The imp scrambled out of his reach and everyone jumped up out of their seats. Triton and Fuzz were running to the imp's assistance when Darius suddenly pulled his hammer from his tool belt and smashed it down on the table.

"The next man to try that will get my hammer in his skull," he said.

At that even Rufius stopped smirking. He seemed to suddenly realize the flaw in his plan: he hadn't brought any knights along to protect him. He slowly got up from his chair and tried to maintain his dignity as he proceeded from the hall, hugging the wall and keeping as far away from Darius as possible.

The delegates ignored their dignity and sprinted after him.

Athena dropped back into her chair and put her head in her hands.

Fuzz rushed over to her and laid a hand on her shoulder. "Don't worry, old girl. We'll think of something." He stared around at the other imps in desperation.

"Nets," said Nikki. "Fishing nets."

Athena took her head out of her hands.

Nikki was startled to see that she'd been crying. It seemed impossible in someone so stiff-backed and steel-willed. She patted Athena's hand. "We collect every fishing net in ImpHaven. When a knight rides by we throw the net over him and pull him off his horse. If we do it right it should tangle him up in a snarled mess. He won't be able to cut himself free if we're quick enough. As soon as he hits the ground we'll grab his sword. Then we just wrap some ropes around the net to tie him up."

"That might work," said Triton, nodding thoughtfully. "It will take some coordination, but leave that to me. I'll round up every fisherman and every member of the Watch. It sounds like the knights have orders to separate and ride through the countryside. That makes our job easier, as each one will be on his own. I'll send messengers out to each village. They know the back ways and shortcuts. Even on foot they'll likely arrive before the knights. ImpHaven doesn't have many roads, so the knights will find their progress much slower than riding along the Realm's royal highways or Kingston's stone streets. I suspect more than a few of them will get lost in our forests."

"You'll need wagons," said Aunt Gertie. "To dump the ruffians in and to transport them once you catch them. I suggest we bring them all back to the city. We'll lock 'em in the potato cellar under the Farmers' Guildhall. It has good stone walls and a stout door with a heavy iron lock. Impossible to get out of. I should know. I got locked in there once as a child when playing hide and seek."

"Athena and me'll round up every farmer and shopkeeper in town who owns a wagon," said Fuzz.

"I'll go talk to Griff and her crew," said Nikki. "I'm sure they'll want to help."

"No, Miss," said Athena. "It is too dangerous for you to be wandering around the docks. You must stay here. This building is very secure once its doors and windows are barred."

Nikki folded her arms and was about to object when Darius cut in.

"I'll go with her," he said. "I suspect any knights we encounter will avoid me, at least for now. The imps make easier prey."

Nikki shoved back her chair and hurried from the hall before Athena could object.

"Are Gwen and Linnea safe?" she asked as they rushed down the front steps of the building and out onto the boardwalk. "And Curio?"

"I think so," said Darius. "They ran toward the house of Athena's mother. It's high up in the hills and has a good view of the lands all around. They should be able to see any attackers long before they arrive."

They hurried down the boardwalk along the harbor, keeping a sharp eye out. They saw no sign of the delegation or the knights. They didn't see any imps either. It was as if the city was deserted. As they passed a fishing boat Nikki suddenly stopped.

"Wait!" she said. She jumped onto the deck of the boat, nearly falling as she slipped on a pile of slimy fish guts. She caught her balance and ran to the stern, where a neatly coiled fishing net lay next to the anchor. She grabbed it with both hands. "Oh my gosh!" she exclaimed. She couldn't even lift it. This wasn't the transparent, nearly weightless fishing line she was used to back in Wisconsin. This was a net used for deep-sea fishing, woven from thick strands of rope.

Darius jumped aboard. "Here, let me," he said, grunting a bit as he lifted the net and threw it over his shoulder. "I hope there are lighter nets in ImpHaven," he said as he struggled to climb out of the boat. "No imp will be able to lift this alone. They'll have to work in groups. Still, it's a good thing to have with us. I was not looking forward to facing down a sword-carrying knight and me without a weapon."

"You could throw your hammer at them," said Nikki as they headed to the Black Boar.

Darius shook his head. "I'm a good man in a fist fight, but my aim is not the best. Never was much good at archery or darts. I'd likely miss the knight and break some shopkeeper's window, or worse, hit an imp. No, your plan for using the nets seems a better idea."

The Black Boar was quiet as they approached, its shutters closed and barred. Nikki ran up the steps and tried the door. It was locked. She banged on it with her fist. "Griff! Kira! Open up. It's me and Darius!"

The lock rattled and the door opened an inch. A sliver of Krill's face showed. When he saw them he quickly pulled them inside and locked the door again. He slid the knife he'd been holding back into a scabbard on his belt.

As they entered the common room a large group of imps stared silently back at them. No one was drinking or gambling and the fire in the stone fire pit had been doused. The black-bearded imp who'd taken Krill's money in yesterday's dice game was watching them as he tossed a pair of dice in the air and caught it.

"C'mon," said Krill. "Griff's upstairs."

They climbed a set of creaky wooden stairs to the upper floor of the pub. A long hallway stretched the length of the building. Krill led them into a room overlooking the harbor. Griff was seated at a table staring at a map. Kira was looking out the window.

"Nikki!" said Kira, rushing over. "You're safe! Any news? An imp ran into the pub half an hour ago shouting that knights in full armor were invading ImpHaven. At first we thought he was drunk, but he described a charge by the knights across the Roaring River. Said he'd seen it with his own eyes. Tarn went out to see what's going on."

"Yes, there's been an invasion," said Nikki. "While Rufius was distracting us the Knights of the Iron Fist crossed the old stone bridge over the Roaring River. The knights are spreading across the countryside, herding the imps into the city. We . . ."

Nikki stopped abruptly. The pounding of a horse's hooves could be heard echoing along the boardwalk outside.

Griff shoved back her chair and hurried to the window. "A knight," she said. "Looks like he's alone."

Nikki dashed over and carefully peered over the windowsill. Directly below them an armored knight had dismounted from his horse and was tying it to a wooden post. Nikki waved frantically at Darius. "The net," she whispered.

Darius nodded.

Nikki eased the shutters farther open, careful to make no sound.

Darius pulled the net off his shoulder and leaned out. He took careful aim and dropped the net.

A startled shout came from below as the net hit its target. The knight tripped and fell to his knees.

"Hurry!" said Darius, motioning to Krill. They dashed from the room, Nikki and Kira on their heels.

When they reached the netted knight he'd almost managed to free himself. Krill tackled him and they went down in a clash of armor and a tangle of net. Darius pulled his hammer from his tool belt and watched for an opening. The knight grunted and swore and fought furiously but he was hampered by his bulky armor. Darius waded in and brought his hammer down on the knight's helmet. A bell-like clang rang out and the knight dropped like a stone.

Krill climbed to his feet, breathing hard.

"Do you see any others?" said Griff, looking down at them from the window.

Kira looked up and down the boardwalk. "No. The knights seem braver here than they were in Kingston. There it was rare to see one on his own."

A small crowd of imps poured out of the pub and stood looking down at the unconscious knight.

The black-bearded imp walked up and spat on him. "We'll stick him in me root cellar," he said. "Got a pile of rotten parsnips in there giving off a lovely smell. I'm sure he'll enjoy that. Specially if we rub his face in them." He pulled the bar off of a cellar door built into the foundations of the pub.

Darius and Krill carried the knight down into the cellar. When they reappeared Darius was carrying the net.

"Got some rope to tie him up with?" asked Krill.

The imp nodded. "Leave that to us. We'll wrap 'im up nice and tight. And if you catch any more of these marauders send 'em along. Lots of room in me cellar."

Chapter Six

The Defense of ImpHaven

NIKKI TRUDGED ALONG the forest track, limping a little from a blister on her heel. Her worn-out Nikes made a slapping sound as she walked. One of the soles had detached from the shoe. Gwen had tried to mend it for her by melting the sole over last night's camp fire, but it had come loose again.

"I'll have another look at that when we stop," said Gwen, looking back over her shoulder. "It'll be hard to sneak up on any knights with you flapping like that."

"I have a spare pair of boots in my cabin on our ship," said Kira, who was walking behind Nikki. "If we ever get back to town they're yours."

"Thanks," said Nikki, adjusting the net which hung across her shoulder. Gwen and Kira were also carrying nets. These were lighter than the deep-sea net Darius had dropped on the knight back at the Black Boar. They were made of strands of twisted cotton rather than rope. Imp women used them to catch salmon in the Roaring River. Nikki was grateful for their lightness but she was worried the nets wouldn't be up to the task of tangling a knight. To compensate their plan was to throw all three nets onto any knight they came across.

"No sightings yet, Misses," said Curio, running up to them. He'd been scouting ahead, with firm orders to hide behind a tree if he spotted any knights.

They were searching the pine forests of central ImpHaven for stray knights. The area was a day's walk from the city of ImpHaven and not many imps lived in the forest. Their chances of coming across a knight were pretty low, much to Curio's disappointment.

Nikki had tried to leave him behind at Athena's mother's house, which was being used as a headquarters. She was terribly worried that his impulsiveness would get him hurt or even killed. She'd had to leave Cation behind with Athena's mother and she'd tried to convince Curio to stay and look after the kitten, but he'd stubbornly refused.

He'd also refused to stay and help Linnea, who was converting the house to a makeshift field-hospital. She'd set up cots inside the downstairs dining room with a small group of imps who had experience tending wounds and other injuries. They hadn't had any injured imps arrive yet, though reports had started to come in from the countryside of imps hurt while fleeing the knights. No fatalities had been reported, though there were nasty rumors of the knights setting fire to crops and cottages. Most of the injuries among the imps were minor things like broken legs caused by running away in panic. The knights seemed intent on clearing the countryside of imps rather than killing them.

Athena's mother had setup a command center in the parlor of her house and she and Aunt Gertie were in charge of sending out search parties. Darius and Krill, as the only men in the defense of ImpHaven, were each sent out alone to hunt along the banks of the Roaring River, where the largest number of knights had been spotted. Aunt Gertie had divided all the imps who were part of the Watch into groups of six and sent them into the farmlands closest to town. They carried the lighter cotton nets. Groups of fishermen consisting of ten imps each were sent to the small fishing villages along the sea coast. Each group carried two heavy deep-sea fishing nets. Athena and Fuzz had gone out to help the scouts, who sent any knight-sightings back to

Headquarters by carrier pigeons. Griff and her crew were patrolling the sea coast on their ship, watching for any invasion by sea.

No one knew where Rufius and his delegates were hiding. They'd never returned to their ship and seemed to have vanished into thin air. At first there'd been hope that the Knights of the Iron Fist might abandon their invasion if Rufius wasn't around to give orders, but the knights continued their rampage across the countryside. They seemed to be following a plan that had been thought out in advance of the invasion. They were methodically driving imps out of the countryside and herding them into the town of ImpHaven.

"I wonder if any more knights have crossed the river," said Kira, shifting her net to her other shoulder.

Gwen groaned. "Don't even say that. We have enough of them to deal with as it is."

"Sorry," said Kira. "I was just wondering how many of them have crossed into ImpHaven. No one really knows how many members of the Knights of the Iron Fist there actually are. The Prince of Physics had them counted once, last year. But he only counted the ones in Kingston. There were two hundred and ten. Not a huge number, but each knight is a threat because of his armor, his sword, and his horse. One armed knight can run down a large crowd of unarmed people who're on foot."

"There are several hundred in Deceptionville," said Gwen. "But they tend to keep a low profile. The merchants don't like them, and money rules in Deceptionville. I suspect the merchants bribe the knights to stay out of city politics. The Rounders keep a sharp eye on them and chuck them in jail if they start throwing their weight around. No one in D-ville seems to have copied Rufius in bribing them to become his personal army."

"I'm surprised Fortuna or Avaricious haven't tried that," said Nikki.

"It's not really their style," said Gwen. "Those two have one-track minds. It's all about money with them. They aren't as obsessed with power as Rufius seems to be. Fortuna's take-over of D-ville's City Hall is more about channeling tax money into her personal coffers than it is about ordering people around. She's too lazy to be a dictator. Same with Avaricious."

"Miss, are we going to stop soon?" Curio asked Nikki. "I'm so hungry I could eat a squirrel."

Gwen laughed. "You might have to," she said. "We ate too much of our rations last night. We . . ."

"Sshhh!" hissed Kira, coming to a sudden halt. She held up a hand.

They all stopped, listening intently.

Voices could be heard ahead of them, drifting on the wind. Many high-pitched voices.

"It sounds like a large group of imps," whispered Gwen.

Kira nodded. "Yes. And I can hear horses' hooves as well."

Nikki's hands tightened on her net. She was about to motion Curio to get behind them when he suddenly took off, running toward the voices. Nikki swore under her breath and ran after him, followed closely by Kira and Gwen.

When they caught up with Curio he was hiding behind a large rhododendron bush at the edge of a clearing. They crouched down beside him and peered out through the leaves.

A large group of more than thirty imps was huddled together on the grass. Circling them was a single knight on horseback. His sword was out and he rode slowly around and around them, angling in toward any who seemed on the verge of making a run for it. There were both men and women in the group and some of them had small children clinging to their backs.

Gwen slowly sat down on the ground behind the bush and motioned to the others to do the same. They sat and watched as she quietly pulled her rucksack off her back and opened it. She pulled out a small glass jar filled with what looked like vegetable oil. A piece of grayish metal floated in the oil. Then she pulled out a water flask and a small wooden bowl. She poured the water into the bowl and opened the glass jar, carefully pulling out the gray piece of metal.

She leaned close to Nikki and whispered in her ear. "Potash."

"Oh!" whispered Nikki, nodding to show that she understood. She pulled her net off her shoulder and motioned to Kira to do the same.

Gwen crouched behind the bush, watching as the knight circled the group of imps. There was an agonizing pause when the horse suddenly decided it was hungry and dropped its head down to the grass at its feet. A dead silence fell in the clearing, broken only by the grinding of the horse's teeth.

Growing impatient, the knight jerked on the reins and the horse ambled on again. When the horse and rider finally reached their bush Gwen jumped up and ran into the clearing, holding the bowl of water. Before the startled knight had time to react she dropped the grayish metal into the bowl of water and thrust it under the horse's nose. Flames suddenly shot out of the water, straight at the horse. The horse reared in fright, its front hooves beating the air.

The knight toppled from the horse's back with a loud yell. Nikki and Kira rushed forward and threw their nets over him, hanging onto the edges of the nets to try and pin him down. To their dismay the knight had the presence of mind not to drop his sword. He slashed at the nets and almost managed to free himself. Nikki ducked as a sword blow passed so close it scratched her cheek.

Gwen and Curio both threw themselves on top of the knight, trying to wrestle his sword from him. It would have gone very badly for them if the imps had not suddenly rushed forward as a group and piled themselves on top of the knight. With six imps sitting on his sword arm and another ten on his legs the knight finally dropped his weapon.

It was still a bit of a wrestling match, as the knight fought even without a weapon, but they finally managed to wrap him up tightly in all three nets. Everyone backed off and plopped down on the grass, trying to catch their breath while the knight lay on the grass like a very badly wrapped Christmas present.

"What *was* that?" asked Kira, staring at the bowel Gwen had dropped.

"Potash," said Gwen. "It's mined in the Haunted Hills. You can extract a silvery metal from it which explodes in water. You have to keep it in vegetable oil to prevent it from reacting with the air." She laughed at Kira's alarmed expression. "Don't worry. I used up all I had with me. My rucksack isn't going to suddenly catch on fire. And it's not magic. It's actually a fairly common substance. Nikki for one has seen it before."

Nikki nodded. "Yes, we call it potassium in my world. My teacher showed us how it explodes in water. If you don't keep it in oil it reacts with a substance in the air called oxygen and can explode. When you drop it in water the reaction pulls hydrogen from the water to create hydrogen gas, which causes the explosion." She looked over at the imps, who were eyeing them warily. They seemed almost as afraid of them as they were of the knight.

She stood up and gathered Gwen's bowl and glass jar. "Curio, why don't you see if you can collect the knight's horse. It's over there at the edge of the clearing. We can use it to carry the knight."

Curio ran off to have words with the horse, which was munching on a tuft of grass.

"Um, what's the plan?" asked Kira, looking at the imps. "Do we just leave them here?"

Gwen shook her head. "I don't think so. I think it would be better to send them on to town. I know it seems strange to follow the same plan as the knights, but they'll be safer in the city."

"I agree," said Nikki. She approached one of the older imps, a tough-looking imp wearing a blacksmith's leather apron. "Excuse me sir, but we would like you all to head for the city of ImpHaven. Are you familiar with the names Athena and Fuzz? The King's Emissaries?"

The imp nodded, giving her a sharp but not unfriendly stare.

"Well, the house of Athena's mother is being used as Headquarters," said Nikki. "The entire country of ImpHaven is under attack by the Knights of the Iron Fist. If you can reach Headquarters they'll find lodging for you, and possibly assign you to search parties if some of you want to help fight the knights."

The imp nodded again. Murmurs of approval came from the other imps.

Nikki glanced down at the trussed-up knight. He glared at her from inside the tangle of nets. "Curio, would you bring the horse over?"

"Yes, Miss," said Curio, dragging the somewhat reluctant horse over by its reins. Its nose whiskers were singed from Gwen's potash fire, but otherwise it seemed unharmed.

"Are you willing to take him to the city with you?" Nikki asked the imp. "They have a secure place there where he'll be locked up."

The imp looked down at the knight with a dangerous light in his eyes.

The hair on the back of Nikki's neck stood up. "You're not going to drop him in the nearest lake, are you?" she asked.

The imp grinned nastily, but shook his head. "No, Miss. We won't drown 'im. Not in lake nor river."

"And you're not going to cut his throat?"

The imp grinned again and didn't answer.

"Maybe we should take him with us," said Nikki to Gwen and Kira.

"We can't cart him all over the countryside," said Kira. "Taking him back to the city is the best option." She turned to the imp. "Take him to the Harbormaster. He has a jail set up for captured knights."

The imp nodded, an unpleasant smile still flickering across his face.

Nikki looked at him uneasily, but she didn't have a better suggestion. "What are we going to do about the nets?" she asked Kira. "We're going to need them, and we don't have any rope to tie the knight up with."

The imp spoke up. "Plenty of nets in our village. Made of strong twine. We use 'em to catch trout in Lost Lake. It's not far from here. Stay on the path through the woods, that way, and you'll soon come to it. Take anything you need."

Nikki still didn't like the idea of leaving the trussed-up knight alone with the imps, many of whom looked understandably angry and vengeful, but she bowed to necessity. With help from Gwen and a few of the larger imps she and Kira managed to drag the netted knight up onto the horse's saddle. They laid him sideways across it with his head and feet dangling.

They stood in the clearing watching the procession of imps disappear down the forest path in the direction of ImpHaven City. The horse plodded along, its reins held by the imp in the blacksmith's apron. He turned and gave them a last unpleasant grin and then the imps were gone.

"Well, that was exciting," said Gwen, putting her rucksack back on. "Come on. It's getting dark. Let's hurry to their village. I'd rather sleep in an imp bed even if it's too small than spend another night on the ground."

They hurried along the path and after only a mile or two came to the outskirts of a small village. It was a cluster of whitewashed cottages along the sandy shoreline of a lake. Vegetable gardens were planted behind the cottages and several cows chewed their cud in the middle of a pasture. It was eerily quiet, with only an occasional moo to break the stillness.

As they walked along the lake they saw that the knight had been busy. All the doors of the cottages were smashed in and two of the cottages had been burned to the ground, their ashes still smoldering.

Gwen went up to the burned cottages and felt a heap of ash with her palm. The pile crumbled, revealing red-hot coals underneath. "We'd better douse these," she said. "If the wind picks up the fire could spread to the other buildings."

They found wooden buckets in a shed in someone's garden and spent the next hour dumping lake water onto the fires. By the time they were finished they were all exhausted and the sun had set. They picked the cottage with the least damage and pushed through its smashed front door. The ceilings were so low they had to stoop, but the interior was undamaged and the walls were sturdy. Nikki and Kira barricaded the front door with chairs and a wooden bench while Gwen and Curio searched the pantry for food.

"A pretty good haul," said Gwen, dumping a rind of cheese, a bag of apples, and some dried pears on the kitchen table. She lit a candle with a piece of flint.

"Do you think that's a good idea?" asked Kira, looking at the reflection of the candle in the crude glass of the window. "What if there are other knights about? It'd be better not to announce that we're here."

Gwen shrugged. "The knights seem pretty organized. My guess is that our knight was assigned to this particular part of the countryside. I doubt another one is going to arrive in this same village."

"Okay," said Kira, though she still looked worried.

Nikki wasn't sure who was right but she was too tired and hungry to worry about it. She took the slice of cheese Gwen offered and wolfed it down. It was tangy and very salty. "Anything to drink?" she asked, coughing.

Gwen shook her head. "Nothing but lake water. I wouldn't recommend drinking that. I saw cow tracks going down into the lake from the beach. My guess is they water the cows by just leading them into the lake. Drinking from it might make you sick."

Curio jumped up. "Milk," he said. "I'll milk the cows. I know how. When my master in D-ville didn't feed me I used to go out to the cow pastures on the edge of town and milk the cows for my supper." He ran to the door and started pulling at their barricade.

"I'll go with him," said Nikki. She grabbed a broom which was propped against the wall and followed Curio out into the night.

The night was cloudy and the moon was only a pale sliver low on the horizon. Tall pines surrounded the cow pasture, casting deep black shadows. Nikki picked her way across the damp grass, trying to smell the cow patties before she stepped in them. Curio found a tin bucket in a nearby shed and approached the nearest cow, gently patting its nose. The cow sniffed at him curiously but was content to let him milk her.

Nikki kept a firm grasp on the broom handle, but the night seemed still and peaceful. The only sound was an owl hooting softly in one of the pines and the quiet grinding of the cows chewing their cud. It was only when Curio had finished with the first cow and moved onto the next that a noise made Nikki stand to attention. She squinted at the darkness under the pines. A blackness moved in the shadows. Nikki sucked in her breath and moved closer to Curio, grasping her broom like a baseball bat.

Something moved out from under the trees and showed itself in the dim light of the pasture. At first Nikki thought it was a large dog, but somehow the shape was wrong.

"It's a wolf, Miss," said Curio, barely glancing up from his milking. "It's probably after the cows. Don't run."

"Okay," said Nikki as calmly as she could considering her heart was trying to climb up into her throat. "What's the plan? I don't have any experience with wolves."

"They startle easily," said Curio. "Give me your broom."

Nikki handed it to him and he whacked it against the side of his tin pail. The clanging sound rang across the pasture. The wolf yelped and jumped backwards, disappearing back into the forest.

Curio calmly handed the broom back to her and set about milking the second cow. "Came across the occasional wolf back in old D-ville," he said. "On the outskirts. They were there for the same reason I was. To get at the cows. Wolves usually won't bother you, though you gotta watch out for bears. I used to hear stories of bear attacks in the Mystic Mountains. Never been there meself, but I hear they have a really large type of bear which sometimes attacks people. Best to stay out of those mountains. Very strange stories come outta there."

Nikki nodded, thinking of the citadel high up in the Mystic Mountains and the hot-air balloon she'd escaped in. She wondered where the citadel dwellers were now. They'd left on a rampage, determined to kill the King, and in all the chaos caused by the knights she'd forgotten to tell anyone about them. She'd have to tell Athena about them as soon as they returned to ImpHaven City.

"That should do it, Miss," said Curio, giving the cow a pat on its haunches. "Full pail."

"Here," said Nikki, handing him the broom and lifting the heavy pail. She glanced around the pasture. "Do you think we ought to put these cows in one of the sheds? In case the wolf comes back?"

"Nah," said Curio. "I seen a cow kick a wolf once. It flew up in the air and hit a tree. If the wolf comes back this lot'll bunch together and start kicking."

"Wonderful," said Gwen as they set the full pail on the table. "That plus the cheese should keep us going for a while. Tomorrow morning we'll search the rest of the cottages for supplies. We need all the food we can find, as our assigned path takes us deeper into the forest. We may have trouble finding food." She pulled a piece of wrinkled parchment out of the pocket of her blacksmith's apron.

They all leaned into the candlelight as Gwen traced a finger along the map Aunt Gertie had drawn for them.

"We're getting close to the Southern Mountains," said Gwen. "I've never been to ImpHaven before, but I had a tutor who taught me geography when I was a child. We covered the Realm and its bordering lands pretty thoroughly. The Southern Mountains form the southern border of ImpHaven. Beyond them lie the Barren Plains. Few people from the Realm have ever been to the Plains. They're mostly unpopulated. Just a few tribes of nomadic sheep herders. There's no reason for the Knights of the Iron Fist to go there, so once we reach the foothills of the mountains we need to decide what to do. Kira, have you ever travelled in ImpHaven?"

Kira shook her head, her long braids dancing. "Nope. We've sailed into the port at ImpHaven City a few times. That's all."

"Well," said Gwen, studying the map. "According to this there are only two more villages between us and the Southern Mountains. I think this squiggly line here is the forest path we've been following. There don't seem to be any roads in this part of the country. I say we stay on the path, check out the next two villages, and then head west toward the Roaring River and follow it back to ImpHaven City."

Curio looked disappointed. "But Miss, we've only bagged one knight. Maybe we should turn east toward the coast instead. This maps shows more villages along there. I bet there'll be more tin-heads in that area."

Gwen shook her head. "Griff and her crew are covering the coast. Our orders are to cover this part of the forest."

Curio looked mutinous, but Gwen gave him a stern glance. "I'm the eldest here and I feel a certain responsibility to get all of you back safely. If we find any more knights we'll do our best to deal with them, but we aren't going to go looking for trouble. Also, I suspect Aunt Gertie assigned us this area because it's less populated and therefore likely to have fewer knights. None of you are of age yet and she doesn't want you hurt. Now eat up and let's get to bed. We've got a long trek ahead of us tomorrow."

Chapter Seven

The Conclave

NIKKI GROANED. HER back was stiff and her knees felt like they would never straighten out again. Kira and Gwen were also grumbling. A night spent in tiny imp beds had bent everyone out of shape except for Curio. His size had saved him from being twisted into a pretzel. He ran along the path ahead of them, trying to catch a dragonfly buzzing around his head.

They'd stuffed their rucksacks full of wheels of cheese and bags of dried fruit. The weight plus the burden of the nets made for slow going. It took them all day to reach the next imp village, a tiny hamlet beside a rocky creek. The cottages were again ransacked, with all the doors and windows smashed. No food had been left in the pantries and they found no personal belongings. No clothes or candlesticks or pottery. This gave them some hope that the imps had escaped before the knights arrived.

Gwen stopped on the bank of the creek to consult the map. "I say we push on to the next village and spend the night there. According to the map these two villages are fairly close together. Shouldn't be more than another hour or two."

Nikki and Kira nodded wearily and they continued their trudge along the forest path. Nikki tried to distract herself from her sore feet and aching back by admiring the beauty of the woods. The setting sun was turning the sky red above the tops of the pines and purple rhododendrons shone in the gloom at the roots of the trees. A blue jay squawked somewhere in the branches.

"What's that rushing sound?" Nikki asked, pausing to listen. "It sounds like thunder."

"It must be the Roaring River," said Gwen, checking the map. "We're getting close to the mountain pass where the river rushes down a series of huge waterfalls called the Stairway to the Clouds. I remember my tutor telling me that the Roaring River is the swiftest river in the Realm. It has a huge current flow in both speed and volume and the crashing of water down the Stairway can be heard for miles."

Another hour of walking brought them to the last village before the mountains. The final rays of the setting sun warmed them briefly as they emerged from the forest into a small pasture. They crossed the wet grass of the pasture into the village. A large cluster of whitewashed cottages huddled around a village green, a patch of lawn with a pond in the middle and sheep grazing on the grass. They stood listening for a moment.

"I don't hear anything," said Gwen. "No voices. Neither of imp nor knight." She squinted into the growing darkness. "The doors and windows of the cottages look unbroken. I suppose the imps escaped, but I wonder why the knights didn't rampage and destroy as they did in the last two villages?"

"Hard to say," said Kira. "Maybe they got word to move on to another part of ImpHaven. Aunt Gertie said they've been communicating by carrier pigeon. Maybe they got new orders."

Gwen shook her head, looking worried. "Let's do a careful search before settling in for the night. I don't want to be taken by surprise."

They searched every cottage, shed, and outhouse, but found no one. The only living things left in the village were the sheep on the village green and a pen full of white geese who were honking behind one of the cottages.

Gwen opened the pen and let the geese out. They waddled to the green and started pecking at the grass. "Geese make great watchdogs," she said. "If anyone approaches the village during the night they'll start honking." She led the way across the green to the largest cottage. Its heavy oak front door was taller than the doors of the other cottages. When they stepped inside they were happy to find that the ceilings were taller too.

"Must belong to the village headman," said Kira, dumping her net and rucksack on the polished table in the dining room. "It's great to be able to stand up straight in one of these imp houses." She picked up a pewter mug from the mantelpiece above the fireplace. "Nice metalwork. This village seems richer than the others we've passed through."

"They probably do some mining," said Gwen. "The Southern Mountains have large deposits of tin and a bit of silver." She closed the front door and turned its heavy iron key in the lock. She picked up a tall silver candlestick from the dining table. "I don't think we should light any candles tonight. In the other villages it was clear that the knights had been there, done their destroying, and left. I'm not sure what happened here. If the imps left on their own why didn't they take their valuables?"

Nikki and Kira shrugged.

"Look what I found!" said Curio, darting out of the pantry. He held up a small wooden cask with a cork in the top. "Ale!"

"Give me that," said Gwen. She took the cask from him and set it on the table. "You're far too young to be drinking ale."

"But Miss," said Curio, "there's nothing else to drink except a pitcher of spoiled milk. There ain't any cows in the pasture. They must've run off when the imps left. Can't get no more milk. Besides, Fuzz drinks ale all the time. Never does him no harm."

"Fuzz is an adult and can drink what he wants," said Gwen.

"You're just a child."

Curio looked up at her with puppy-dog eyes, his perpetual smile turned down in a pout.

Gwen rolled her eyes. "All right. Stop laying on the guilt. But you're only having one small mug. Go see if there are any dishes in the pantry."

Curio saluted and ran back into the pantry where they heard him crashing around.

"There are four bedrooms," said Nikki, returning from an exploration of the cottage. "Nice tall ceilings and beds long enough for us to stretch out in."

Gwen nodded. "Okay, but let's double up. It'll be safer. I'll keep Curio with me and you two bunk together. Make sure your windows are locked."

✦ ✦ ✦ ✦

NIKKI WOKE SUDDENLY. She sat up in bed, looking wildly around the strange bedroom, uncertain for a moment where she was. A snore from Kira brought her back to her senses. She squinted at the diamond-paned window which looked out over the village green. It was still pitch-black outside. She yawned and rubbed her forehead. She had a splitting headache, probably from the mug of ale she'd had. She'd never drunk ale before, or beer for that matter. If beer tasted as awful as ale then her mother had nothing to worry about. When she got to college she was sticking to Mountain Dew at college parties.

Gwen and Kira had both had three mugs of ale each, which probably explained why Kira was fast asleep and had slept through the noise. Nikki frowned, looking intently around the room. She was sure she'd been woken by a noise. She slid out of bed and padded in her stocking feet to the window. The cottage glass was crude and wavy, but she could just make out a streak of moonlight shining on the pond in the middle of the village green. She could see fuzzy white blobs which were probably sheep. She stood there for a long moment, watching and listening intently. She was just about to go back to bed when a sudden movement caught her eye. She held her breath. Was it just an animal? It seemed to be circling the pond.

She rubbed at the dusty glass with the sleeve of her tunic. She could see the thing more clearly now. It was too tall for a wolf. As it stepped into a patch of moonlight she gasped. It was a man.

Nikki dashed to the bed and shook Kira.

"What?" groaned Kira. "Go away." She pulled the bedspread over her head.

"Wake up!" hissed Nikki. "There's someone out by the pond!"

Kira pulled off the covers and sat up. "Are you sure? Oh, my head. Now I remember why Griff doesn't let me drink ale."

"Never mind your head!" whispered Nikki. "Come and look!"

Kira stumbled to the window. "I don't see anything."

"Wait," said Nikki, her nose to the glass. "There! See? He's standing next to that sheep. I don't think it's a knight. If he was the moonlight would shine off his armor. It looks like he's dressed all in black. That's why he's so hard to see."

Kira nodded. "I see him now. Stay here and watch. I'll go wake Gwen and Curio."

Nikki quietly pulled on her Nikes. They'd all slept in their clothes to be ready for emergencies. She wondered if there were any weapons in the cottage. The imps didn't seem to go in for swords, but a fireplace poker might come in handy.

"Let me see," said Gwen, running into the bedroom. She took one look out the window and jumped back as if burned. "Lurker," she said.

Kira gasped. "Are you sure?" She peered out the window again. "What would a Lurker be doing here? They never come into ImpHaven. They don't consider it important enough to bother with."

"Well, they seem to have changed their minds," said Gwen grimly.

"Should we go pound him, Miss?" Curio said, sleepily rubbing his eyes. "I bet the four of us could take him."

"No!" hissed Gwen. "Lurkers are dangerous. They carry long knives which they aren't afraid to stick into people." She tested the window to make sure it was locked. "Curio, go put your shoes on. Be careful not to make any noise. Nikki stay here and keep watch. Kira, come with me. We'll double-check all the locks and see if we can find anything to defend ourselves with."

As Nikki watched the Lurker dropped what looked like a rucksack onto the grass and sat down on it. He was facing away from their cottage and didn't seem aware he was being watched. After a few minutes the others came back into the room. They had their shoes and travel cloaks on. Gwen put Nikki's cloak around her shoulders and handed her a small metal shovel of the kind used to put coals on a fire. Kira dumped their fishing nets on the bed. She and Curio were armed with brooms. Gwen had a long, sharp kitchen knife in her hand. Nikki glanced at the knife and raised an eyebrow, wondering if Gwen was really capable of stabbing someone.

Gwen noticed her glance and shrugged. "I'll cross that bridge when I come to it. I admit I don't think I could kill, but I don't have any qualms about giving the Lurker a nice deep wound in the leg."

Kira and Curio sat down on the bed and Gwen joined Nikki at the window. For a long time nothing happened. The Lurker sat still as a stone while the sky gradually lightened above the tree tops. The rising sun turned the grass around the pond a bright green and a bird started chirping somewhere.

Nikki was leaning against the windowsill, dozing slightly, when she suddenly bolted upright. Gwen laid a hand on her arm and raised a warning hand as Curio started to say something.

Nikki and Gwen watched as a troop of knights in full armor appeared out of the forest. They headed straight for the village green.

The Lurker calmly got to his feet and watched as the knights dismounted and led their horses to the pond to drink. More knights kept coming until there were more than forty gathered on the grass.

Gwen hissed softly as six more Lurkers appeared, all on horseback, all dressed in their usual black cloak and hood. Behind the Lurkers another horse appeared, a big-boned stallion draped in a red velvet saddlecloth with a bridle decorated with tracings of gold. Nikki and Gwen both gasped. On its back sat the grotesquely fat body of Avaricious.

"What on earth!" exclaimed Gwen. "He hasn't been outside of D-ville in years. Decades maybe."

"Look who else is here," said Nikki, pointing at the horse which had just arrived, surrounded by a troop of knights.

Wrapped in a heavy black velvet travelling cloak, with jewels glittering on the collar, was Fortuna the Fortunate.

"My stars, it's a regular conclave," Gwen whispered. "What are they all doing here?"

"A better question is how are we going to get out of here without being seen," said Kira, looking out the window.

Gwen drummed her fingers on the windowsill, lost in thought. Finally she seemed to come to a decision. "The cottage has a back door. It's locked and barred from the inside. I double-checked it myself last night. It looks like they're about to start some kind of meeting. We'll wait until they're deep into their discussions, and then you three will go out the back way. Head into the forest, toward the Roaring River. You'll be able to tell which way to go from the noise of the waterfalls. Follow the river back to ImpHaven City and be careful to stay out of sight until you can make contact with the imps. I'll stay here to find out what the Lurkers and the knights are up to."

Nikki and Kira were both shaking their heads vigorously long before Gwen had finished.

"No way," said Nikki. "We're not leaving you here alone. Kira can take Curio back to the imps. I'll stay here with you."

Curio hopped down off the bed and cross his stick-like arms. "I'm not going nowhere," he said.

Gwen was about to reply when her attention was drawn back to the window. A new group of knights had emerged from the forest. "Darius!" she whispered.

"Krill!" gasped Kira, her nose pressed to the glass.

Nikki squinted through the thick glass. They were right. Darius and Krill were walking next to the knights. Krill's hands were tied behind his back and he was attached to a horse's saddle horn by a long rope. Darius was walking freely, his hands untied.

The new arrivals dismounted and pulled Krill over to a birch tree growing near the pond. They tied him to the tree and left him there. Darius walked on his own over to the pond and sat down on a moss-covered boulder. One of the knights took a water flask from his saddlebag and offered it to Darius. He took a long swig and handed it back.

Gwen pulled Nikki and Kira away from the window. "It's getting light out," she said. "They might spot us through the glass."

Kira paced around the room, tugging frantically on one of her long braids. "What are we going to do? We have to rescue them."

"It doesn't look like Darius needs rescuing," said Nikki.

Gwen glared at her. "We don't know that. Let's not jump to conclusions."

"You saw the same thing I saw," said Nikki. "Krill's tied to a tree while Darius is sitting in comfort being offered something to drink."

Kira folded her arms and looked accusingly at Gwen. There was a long moment of uncomfortable silence.

Nikki could see the struggle on Gwen's face. Gwen and Darius had been flirting since the day they'd met. She knew Gwen didn't want to think badly of him, but the way the knights were treating him was very suspicious.

"Maybe he's playacting," Gwen finally said. "Pretending to be on their side."

Nikki looked at her skeptically. The suggestion seemed out of character for Darius. He was a straightforward guy who liked to quarry stone and hit things with his sledgehammer. Pretending to be someone he wasn't didn't seem in his repertoire.

Gwen seemed to sense what she was thinking. She blushed and began pacing. "Regardless of what's going on with Darius, you three still need to get out of here."

Nikki and Kira ignored her. They both peered around the edge of the window, careful to stay out of sight.

"Darius doesn't have his tool belt anymore," said Nikki.

"See!" said Gwen, still pacing the floor. "What did I tell you? They took it away from him because they don't trust him. They were afraid he'd hit one of them with his hammer the first chance he got."

"Maybe," said Nikki, earning a dirty look from Kira.

"My brother is tied to a tree!" hissed Kira. "Don't talk to me of tool belts!"

Nikki held a finger to her lips, pointing out the window.

Avaricious and Fortuna were standing in the middle of the village green. The knights and Lurkers had dismounted and were grouped around them, listening to Fortuna. She was waving her arms and it looked like she was speaking in a loud voice, but her words didn't quite carry all the way to the cottage. All they could hear was a jumble of sound.

"If we could just hear what they're saying," said Kira in frustration.

Nikki turned her attention from the scene on the grass to the window in front of her nose. Thick diamond-shaped panes of glass were embedded in a metal frame which was attached to the wall of the cottage by iron hinges. The hinges were rusty and Nikki could tell that the slightest movement would cause them to squeak loudly. "Curio," she said quietly, "go into the pantry and see if you can find any cooking oil."

Curio nodded and disappeared, returning in a few minutes with a small clay pot.

Nikki took the pot and lifted its lid. The thick liquid inside smelled vaguely fruity, like olive oil. She dipped her fingers into the oil and rubbed it into the hinges of the window, as well as onto the iron latch in the middle where the window split into two halves. She handed the pot to Kira. Holding her breath, she slowly eased the latch up. A crack opened between the two halves of the window. Nikki grabbed them by the edges before they could swing open all the way. She peered through the crack. No one on the village green had turned in their direction. She let out her breath in relief.

Nikki cupped her hand around her ear to catch more of the sound waves coming in the open window, but it wasn't enough. Fortuna's voice still didn't quite carry all the way to the cottage.

Gwen reached up to the latch and carefully closed the window again. "I have an idea," she said. "I'll be right back."

She returned a few minutes later with a large tin funnel.

"Oh," said Nikki, mentally kicking herself for not having the idea first.

Gwen nodded. "I saw it earlier, in the kitchen. My guess is the imps use it to pour milk from milking pails into smaller jars. It still has a faint smell of raw milk. But it should also work as a makeshift ear trumpet." She carefully opened the window a crack and put the wide end of the funnel on the windowsill. She placed the narrow end against her ear.

Sound waves, thought Nikki as she watched Gwen listening intently. As the sound of Fortuna's voice travelled through the air it created high and low pressure areas called a pressure wave. The funnel didn't amplify the waves, but it helped the listener by collecting the waves and sending them more directly into the ear. Part of the reason an ear trumpet worked is that it reduced background noise, channeling the pressure waves of a specific sound into the listener's ear.

They watched for nearly an hour as Gwen remained at the window, her ear pressed to the funnel. Finally she stood up stiffly and closed the window latch.

"Well," she said, rubbing her lower back. "I think I've got the gist. Fortuna's still speaking, but she's been repeating herself for a while now. I think she just likes the sound of her own voice."

"So what's their plan?" asked Kira. "Why are they all here?"

"Gold," said Gwen, sitting down on the bed. "Apparently there's a new gold deposit which was just discovered in the Southern Mountains, not far from here. And it's in ImpHaven's territory."

"That would explain why Avaricious and Fortuna are here," said Kira. "They're both greedy, gold-loving twits. I've spent my whole life either on the sea or in Kingston, but even in Kingston we've heard stories of their greed. But it doesn't really explain the Lurkers or the Knights of the Iron Fist. I can't see either group doing any actual gold mining. Mining is really hard work."

"Their plan is to make the imps do the actual mining," said Gwen, her face pale with anger. "And they aren't going to pay them either. They plan to take over all of ImpHaven and force the imps into slavery. The Lurkers and the knights have been promised a share of any gold recovered from the mines."

"I wonder how Rufius fits into this," said Nikki. "Did they mention him?"

Gwen shook her head. "No. But my guess is that all the bribes he's been handing out to the Knights of the Iron Fist have been paid for by Fortuna and Avaricious. Rufius doesn't have money of his own. Remember when we first met him back at my mother's house? At Muddled Manor? He admitted he was just the son of a cheese seller from Popularnum."

Nikki stood a moment lost in thought. "So Rufius doesn't really control the Knights of the Iron Fist. Fortuna and Avaricious do. The only real claim to power Rufius has is that he's taken Maleficious's place at the King's court. He's the King's chief advisor. That's what he called himself when he and his delegation arrived in ImpHaven. If we could convince the King to strip Rufius of all power and banish him from Castle Cogent I bet that would really help. Most of the citizens of the Realm are still loyal to the King. At the very least we could stop worrying about Rufius and concentrate on how to prevent Fortuna and Avaricious from enslaving the imps."

"Rufius isn't even here," said Kira impatiently. "Why worry about him now? Let's focus on the problem at hand."

"If we can take Rufius down I think that will lessen the threat from the Knights of the Iron Fist," said Nikki. "My guess is that some of them will remain loyal to him, just because he's personally doled out so much money to them. And as much as I hate to say it, he's kind of a charismatic guy. He attracts followers. But if we can get the knights to split into two groups, one following Rufius and the other following Fortuna and Avaricious then maybe we can play them against each other."

Gwen shook her head vigorously. "If the knights split into two factions and start fighting each other that could mean civil war. The fighting would spill out across all the towns and cities of the Realm. Thousands of people could die."

"But if we don't do something thousands of imps could die," said Nikki. "They won't survive long in the mines. Not as slave labor. I doubt either Fortuna or Avaricious care if the imps are worked to death." She took a deep breath, trying to marshal her arguments just as she had done back home in her debate classes. "I think we should split up. One of us should go to Castle Cogent and try to convince the King to turn against Rufius. One of us should go to Kingston to get help from the Prince of Physics. And one of us should stay here to spy on Fortuna and Avaricious. I volunteer to go to Castle Cogent. I'm pretty sure I can find the way on my own. Plus the King likes me. As a visitor from another land and as a King's Emissary I have a bit of pull. I think Kira should be the one to go to the Prince. She knows him best. And Gwen, you should stay here as a spy."

"But what about me, Miss?" asked Curio, holding his broom on his shoulder like a bayonet. "Should I stay here so I can protect Miss Gwen?"

"No," said Nikki. "You should head for the coast and try to find Griff and her crew. You'll be safe on their ship."

Curio's cheerful face immediately took on a mulish look.

Kira sat on the bed, watching to see what Gwen would say.

Nikki sat down next to her and waited.

Gwen sat still as a stone, looking down at the floor. Finally she looked up. "I hate the thought of splitting up, but I think Nikki's plan is a good one. We can't do anything useful here. There are at least fifty knights and a dozen Lurkers out there. Our nets are useless against such large numbers. The best way to help the imps is by finding allies. The only change I'd make is to send Curio to Castle Cogent instead of to the coast." She held up a hand as Curio let out a whispered cheer and Nikki started to object. "There are no guarantees, but I think the road to Castle Cogent is safer than either staying here or trying to get to Kingston. It's also safer than sending Curio off alone to the coast. It's also safer for you," she said, looking at Nikki. "Your face is on wanted posters all over the Realm. Not to mention your accent. Those things make it difficult for you to interact with people. You never know who might recognize you and turn you in. If Curio travels with you he can talk to people while you hide."

"What about my brother?" asked Kira. "What about Krill? We can't just leave him tied to a tree."

Gwen looked at her sadly. "I think we're going to have to do just that. It will be impossible for us to rescue him. He's too well guarded." She held up a hand when Kira started to object. "I don't think his situation is hopeless. If the knights wanted to kill him they would have done so already, instead of going to the trouble of dragging him all the way here. My guess is they'll hold him as a hostage. Right now I think he's safer than we are."

Kira's face looked like it was involved in its own civil war, but eventually she nodded reluctantly.

"Right," said Gwen, standing up. "Let's get out of here. Everybody put on your cloaks and rucksacks and meet me by the back door."

Chapter Eight

On the Road

ESCAPING FROM THE cottage was easier than Nikki had anticipated. They oiled the hinges of the back door and slipped out without anyone on the village green noticing. As they ran silently across a cabbage patch behind the cottage they could hear Fortuna still addressing the gathering in a loud voice.

When they reached the shelter of the forest surrounding the village they paused and looked back. No one was following them.

"Okay," said Gwen. "We all know what we have to do. Kira, I'd suggest following the foothills of the Southern Mountains until you reach the coast. Here's Aunt Gertie's map. There are no roads to the coast, but it shows a rough path through the forest that loggers use. The distance doesn't seem too far. Maybe a week on foot. That route will be safer than trying to follow the Roaring River, as the land near the river will be crawling with knights."

Kira nodded. "I'll try to meet up with Griff and our crew. Sailing to Kingston will be a lot faster than travelling all the way on foot."

"Nikki," said Gwen, "you and Curio should try to find the Lost Highway. It's an old royal road built during the reign of the current King's great-great-grandfather. It runs all the way along the eastern border of the Realm from the Roaring River to Castle Cogent. It's not used much anymore, and parts of it will likely be covered over with trees and other vegetation, but it's the shortest route to the Castle. The eastern part of the Realm is less populated, but there are a few towns along the Lost Highway, so you should be able to steal food."

"Or beg for it," piped up Curio. "Back in D-ville I'd put on me sad face and limp a bit and old ladies would give me all kinds of food. Pies, cherry pastries, I even got a whole roast chicken once."

Gwen laughed. "Well, then I won't have to worry about you two starving."

"You'll be careful, won't you?" Nikki asked Gwen. "You have the most dangerous job."

"I'll be careful to stay out of sight," said Gwen. "I'm going to hide in the forest during the day and only approach the village at night. There's an empty chicken coop behind the cottage we slept in which may prove useful. I suspect that Fortuna will take that cottage for herself, as it's the largest and most comfortable in the village. If they have meetings in there I may be able to overhear them from the chicken coop."

There didn't seem to be anything more to say, so after a last wave goodbye Nikki and Curio headed into the forest in the direction of the Roaring River. Nikki looked back once, but Gwen and Kira had already disappeared into the trees.

There was no path to follow, which made for rough going through deep piles of pine needles and thorn bushes that tore at their cloaks, but none of it seemed to bother Curio. He walked along, humming quietly, as if he was out for a stroll in a park.

Nikki was much less cheerful. She was glad of Curio's company, but she already missed Kira and Gwen badly. Not to mention Fuzz and Athena. The two imps would have been extremely helpful to have along when it came time to talk to the King. That was, if they ever got all the way to Castle Cogent. Curio was fun to have around, but Nikki was painfully aware of being thrust into the adult role again. She felt responsible for Curio because he was so young, just as she had when they'd traveled together through the Trackless Forest.

All that day they headed toward the roaring sound of the river. As the sun started to dip below the horizon they saw mist rising into the sky, turned red by the setting sun. They were approaching the waterfalls called the Stairway to the Clouds that Gwen had told them about. Just before dark they halted.

"How are we ever going to cross, Miss?" said Curio.

Nikki didn't answer. They were on a bluff overlooking the Roaring River, and the river lived up to its name. At least a hundred yards across, its deep green waters rushed along in a foaming chaos of mist and fast currents.

"Mr. Fuzz mentioned a ford somewhere, where horses could cross," said Curio. "But it must be a long way downstream from here. Even a horse would get swept off its feet here."

Nikki nodded, turning to look upstream. At first glance that direction looked even more hopeless. She could just make out the waterfalls through the mist. Giant stair-steps of granite cloven by raging, tumbling water. She was just about to suggest they head downstream when she spotted something in the river.

"Curio, do you see that?" asked Nikki, pointing. "Something's floating on the water, but the current isn't pushing it downstream. It seems to be going across the river."

Curio squinted into the growing darkness. "Can't quite make it out, Miss. Seems to be a boat of some kind."

"That's impossible," said Nikki. "No boat could go across this river. The current would instantly sweep it downstream."

"Let's go see, Miss," said Curio.

They scrambled down the steep bank, bits of rock and dirt falling on their heads and getting into their shoes. The river had carved a small strip of beach along the bank and they made better time than they had struggling through the forest.

As they got nearer they could see that the object was indeed a boat. It was crossing from the far side of the river. A man was sitting in the stern, holding on to a tiller.

"It's got a rudder for steering," whispered Nikki as they hid behind a thorn bush and watched. "But I don't see what's preventing it from getting swept downstream."

"There's a rope across the river, Miss," whispered Curio, pointing above the man's head. His sharp eyes had spotted what Nikki had missed.

Nikki squinted hard into the darkness. Now that she knew where to look she could just make out the rope. It was about ten feet above the man's head and was tied to trees on both sides of the river. One end of another rope was tied to an iron ring which slid along the first rope. The other end was tied to the boat. It was a reaction ferry. She'd seen one on YouTube once, a reaction ferry that was still in use on the Rhine River somewhere in Switzerland. It was an old technology which used the current of the river to power the boat.

As the boat approached them the man stood up. There was a crunch of gravel and he jumped onto the beach, tying the boat to a log. He climbed the riverbank and disappeared into the trees.

"Now's our chance, Miss," whispered Curio. "Hurry, before he comes back!"

"Can you see anyone on the far bank?" whispered Nikki.

"No, Miss. I think he's alone. Hurry!"

They raced along the beach, the roar of the falls hiding the sound of their footsteps. Curio reached the boat first and jumped in. Nikki untied it from the log, nearly falling into the river as the boat immediately took off. She threw herself at the boat, just managing to get her shoulders over the side of bow. Curio tried to pull her in, but Nikki waved him off. "Grab the tiller!" she shouted. Without the rudder to steady it the boat careened wildly from side to side. Nikki felt like she was on the back of a bucking bronco. The boat started to take on water and Nikki was afraid it was going to tip over. She kicked hard with both legs, trying to propel herself over the side, but it was no use. The sides of the boat were too high. She clung to the side as Curio wrestled with the tiller, throwing his whole body against it.

The boat steadied and the far bank came closer and closer. It looked like they were going to make it until something hit the side of the boat right next to Nikki's head. It was a long, feathered arrow, still quivering.

"Get down!" Nikki yelled.

Curio ignored her, clinging determinedly to the tiller. An arrow whizzed past his head, so close that it ruffled his hair.

Two more arrows hit the sandy beach as the boat reached the far shore and its keel crunched against gravel. Nikki and Curio jumped from the boat and crouched behind it as another arrow thudded into its stern.

"We can't stay here, Miss," said Curio. "He might have ways of signaling to someone on this side of the river."

"Just a few more minutes," said Nikki, watching the last light of the setting sun fade on the horizon. "It'll be pitch black once the sun is gone. Then we'll make a run for the bank." She looked behind her. The beach was wide at that point, with nearly twenty yards of empty space to cross.

They crouched in tense silence. If there was anyone else on their side of the river it was impossible to tell. The roar of the falls hid all noise. No more arrows hit the beach or the boat.

"Now," said Nikki, as the sun disappeared and blackness dropped like a velvet curtain.

They dashed across the sand and hit the steep riverbank at a run. Grasping at exposed roots they pulled themselves up the vertical slope, heaving themselves over the top onto a flat area covered with grass.

"We made it, Miss!" said Curio.

"Shhhh!" hissed Nikki. "Come on."

She ran across the grass, crouching low. She was watching her feet, which was why she didn't see it.

"Ooof!" Nikki was knocked onto her back by the force of the impact.

The horse she'd run into gave an irritated snort and resumed eating the grass.

"Oh, Miss!" exclaimed Curio. "What luck!" He patted the horse's neck. "It must belong to the man who crossed the river."

Nikki picked herself up and gave the horse a dirty look. "By luck I assume you mean we should ride it."

"Of course, Miss," said Curio. "We'll get to Castle Cogent much faster on horseback."

"Do you know how to ride a horse?" asked Nikki.

"Nope!" said Curio cheerfully. "I always wanted to try it, though."

Nikki watched doubtfully as he untied the horse's reins from a thorn bush. The only time she'd ever been on a horse was when Rufius and a band of knights had ordered her, Fuzz, and Athena to leave the Haunted Hills. The knights had put them on horses but kept hold of the reins, leading them like little kids on a fairground pony ride.

She watched as Curio tried to climb onto the horse's back. He was too short to get his leg into the stirrup. The horse just ignored him and kept chewing the grass.

Nikki sighed. "Here," she said. "Step into my hand." She cupped her hands and boosted Curio into the saddle.

"Hand me the reins, Miss. I'll steer."

Nikki thought it more likely that the horse was going to do the steering, but she passed the reins over the horse's head and handed them to Curio. She stuck her foot into the stirrup and managed to get up onto the horse without too much trouble. She and Curio both fit into the saddle. "Now what?" she asked.

"Well, we have to get it started, Miss," said Curio. He gave an experimental tug at the reins.

The horse ignored him and stared chewing at the leaves on a thorn bush.

"It seems hungry, Miss," said Curio.

"I don't think that was the right command," said Nikki. "You have to get its attention." She kicked the heels of her Nikes against the horse's flanks.

The horse didn't even flinch.

"Maybe we have to talk its language, Miss," said Curio. He tried clicking his tongue. When that got no response he launched into a long series of guttural noises which sounded more like a wounded sea lion than a horse.

The horse's ears swiveled toward him, as if wondering what on earth was sitting on its back, but it didn't move.

Nikki sighed. "I have an idea." She slid off the horse's back and pulled the reins over its head. She grasped them with both hands and tugged. "Come on horse. We need to get going."

The horse kept chewing.

"We can't stay here all night arguing with this blasted horse," said Nikki. "We need to get out of here. Let's just walk."

"Try one more time, Miss," said Curio. "Pull a bit harder." He patted the horse's neck. "It seems like a good horse. It just needs a bit of encouragement."

Nikki dug her heels into the dirt and leaned back, pulling on the reins as hard as she could. She was so certain that the horse would never move that when it did she fell over.

Once in motion the horse suddenly seemed to decide that it was in a hurry. It launched into a trot with Curio bouncing wildly up and down on its back.

"Hurry, Miss!" he called. "I can't stop it!"

Nikki picked herself up and ran after them, tripping on grassy tussocks and getting tangled in thorn bushes. She ran as fast as she could, but the horse remained just out of reach. It was only when it reached a steep, pine-covered hillside that she managed to catch up. She made a grab for the saddle horn and managed to wrestle herself onto the horse's back, stomach first. She shifted around until she was sitting behind Curio in the saddle.

"I think it's slowing to a walk, Miss," said Curio as the horse headed up the hill.

"Great," said Nikki, trying to catch her breath.

"It seems to know where it's going," said Curio.

"That's good," said Nikki. "Because we certainly don't."

End of Book Five

Nikki's adventures in the Realm of Reason continue in the sixth book of the *Logic to the Rescue* series: *Wizard of the Winds.*

The Logic to the Rescue series

Logic to the Rescue

The Prince of Physics

The Bard of Biology

Mystics and Medicine

The Sorcerer of the Stars

The Hamsters Rule series

Hamsters Rule, Gerbils Drool

Hamsters Rule the School

Excerpt from *Hamsters Rule, Gerbils Drool*

Chapter One

MELVIN STIRRED UNEASILY in his pile of sawdust shavings. The snuffly snores coming from the twin bed across the room were disturbing his rest. He crawled out of his nest and trundled down an orange plastic tunnel to a distant corner of his Hamster Habitat. Diving head first into a pile of cedar chips, he squirmed until only his chubby rear-end was visible. He twitched for a few seconds then settled back into sleep.

Melvin should have counted himself lucky. The snores of his owner, Miss Sally Jane Hesslop, who was eleven years old as of last Tuesday, were much quieter than usual due to Sally's head being buried under her *Xena Warrior Princess* bedspread. All that could be seen of Sally was a long strand of blonde hair with a wad of pink bubble gum stuck on the end of it.

The morning sun finished clearing the fog from San Francisco bay and lit up Sally's bedroom window. The light revealed quite a mess: Legos, comic books, sneakers, mismatched socks and a spilled can of Hungry Hamster Snacks were scattered across the floor. Sally was a firm believer in keeping all of her belongings in plain view. In an emergency (and most mornings were an emergency, as Sally had a talent for being late for school) precious time could be saved by getting dressed from the clothes on the floor.

This morning Sally's peaceful slumber was destined to last only a few more brief moments, for Robbie was out of bed and on the loose.

Robbie was Sally's four-year-old brother. He was famous up and down their neighborhood for his ability to eat anything dirt-related. Mud, clay, sand, litter box filler, anything lurking in the bottom of a flowerpot or fish tank, all were fair game. When it came to dirt Robbie was an omnivore. Though, of course, he had his favorites. The light fluffiness at the heart of the vacuum cleaner bag, the tasty compost at the roots of his grandmother's roses – these were special treats for special occasions, to be savored slowly and washed down with a good quality grape Kool Aid.

Today Robbie was up at his usual time of six a.m. He tiptoed into Sally's room, a stealthy menace in his footie pajamas and bike helmet. This helmet was a permanent item in Robbie's wardrobe. Robbie was fond of banging his head on things, so his father had started putting a helmet on him as soon as Robbie got out of bed.

Giggling softly and wielding a large rubber spatula, Robbie crept up to the snoring Sally. He pulled back the edge of the bedspread with one chubby fist and brought the spatula down with a satisfying thwhack on top of Sally's head.

"Aaaah!" Sally bolted upright, her scrawny arms swinging wildly as she tried to ward off her assailant. Her oversized *Xena* T-shirt billowed out, making her eighty-pound frame look twice its size. A yellow post-it note which was stuck to her forehead fluttered in the breeze as she whipped around and grabbed the spatula from a chortling Robbie. Sally rained down a barrage of blows with the spatula onto Robbie's bike helmet. Robbie made a dash for the door, knocking over a stack of comic books. He was almost to safety, inches from escape, when he miscalculated the distance between the door jamb and his head. He bounced backwards off the door, his helmet taking most of the punishment, tripped over a half-built castle made of Legos, and toppled over onto the carpet with his feet in the air.

Sally leapt out of bed with a wild war cry and rained rubbery blows down on Robbie as if beating a stubborn batch of dough.

"Sally Jane, are you out of bed yet?" The voice floating in from the hallway sounded in desperate need of coffee. Sally's father's dearest dream was to sleep in past six a.m., a dream which was destroyed on a daily basis by Robbie and his spatula. Robbie had assigned himself the task of family alarm clock and he took his job seriously. If the first whack on the head didn't wake his target at six on the dot then Robbie would tirelessly whack until he got results. Mr. Hesslop had tried hiding the spatula in the back of the cereal cupboard, but Robbie had just switched to whacking with the toilet brush. Mr. Hesslop had quickly decided that he preferred the spatula, the toilet brush tending to catch in his hair.

Sally gave Robbie one final blow then grabbed his pajama feet and dragged him out of her room. "I'm up, Dad. I'm up," she shouted, leaving Robbie lying on his back in the hallway. Sally darted back into her room and slammed the door. She yawned, scratched her ear with the captured spatula, and surveyed her wardrobe. Her favorite pair of jeans, only slightly muddy around the knees, hung off the end of her bed. She pulled them on and selected a pink T-shirt from a pile under the window. As she pulled it over her head the post-it which was stuck to her forehead fluttered to the floor. Sally scooped it up and read it aloud.

"Charlie Sanderson must pay. Skedyul revenge for recess."

Sally's blue eyes narrowed to slits, and she smacked her palm with the spatula.

"Right. It's payday, Charlie. Today, after third period."

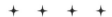

✦ ✦ ✦ ✦

"OKAY, ROBBIE. YOU'VE had enough. Come and drink your juice."

Robbie, crouching over a scraggly fern which an aunt had given them for Christmas, ignored his Dad. He reached into the depths of the flowerpot and pulled up a fistful of loamy soil. He carefully picked off a ladybug which was crawling on his thumb and then crammed the dirt into his mouth.

Mr. Hesslop sighed. He grabbed Robbie off the floor and plopped him into a chair at the kitchen table. Mr. Hesslop was a taller version of Sally Jane. Both father and daughter had dishwater blond hair, blue eyes, long skinny arms and legs, and pointy elbows. Short, chubby Robbie, with his dark hair and brown eyes, looked completely unrelated to his Dad and his eleven-year-old sister, a fact which Sally mercilessly exploited. She had convinced Robbie that he was on loan from the bank that their Dad worked at, and that he could be returned at any time if she just said the word. Robbie had responded to this threat by reducing Sally's spatula wake-up calls to once a week. His Dad still got the seven-day-a-week treatment though. Robbie guessed correctly that his Dad loved him too much to pack him up and lock him in a bank vault.

"Robbie, you've got to stop eating dirt." Mr. Hesslop grabbed a paper napkin and wiped Robbie's muddy mouth. "Remember what Dr. Tompkins told you? If you don't stop you're going to have a tree growing in there." He tickled Robbie's stomach.

Robbie giggled. "Tree in tummy."

Sally wandered into the kitchen, bumping into the refrigerator. Her long, straight hair hung in front of her face like a curtain. She had attempted to braid pieces of it, and the attempt had not gone well. One braid sprouted from the top of her head like an overgrown onion. Another looked like it was growing straight out of her ear. She sat down at the kitchen table, one hand tangled in the rest of her unbraided hair, the other grabbing for a box of Cheerios.

Mr. Hesslop passed her the milk. "Sally Jane, why don't you let me help you with your hair? I'll make you look real pretty."

What could be seen of Sally's face under her hair looked suspiciously like it was rolling its eyes. "Daaad. I'm not trying to look *pretty*. I'm doing Xena braids. See, if you're in a fight you don't want your hair in your face. You can't see good."

"What fight?" Mr. Hesslop said sharply, his thin nose pointed at his daughter like a fox on the scent.

Sally smiled innocently. "I was just being hypometical, Dad. Sheesh."

"Hypothetical," said Mr. Hesslop. "Robbie, don't do that." He grabbed Robbie's juice glass, which was now half empty. Robbie had poured the rest onto the floor and was straining against his father's arm, eager to get down from the table to study (and taste) the effects of orange juice on dirty linoleum at close range.

Melvin waddled into the kitchen, his fluffy orange fur dusting a path along the un-swept floor, his nose twitching for food. He disappeared under Sally's chair, dodged her swinging feet, and settled in front of the puddle of orange juice. His tiny pink tongue darted out and lapped at lightning speed, aware that even Mr. Hesslop with his lazy housekeeping skills was unlikely to leave a bonanza like this lying around for long.

Fortunately for Melvin, Mr. Hesslop was distracted by the sound of a knock at the front door. He set Robbie down and went to greet their visitor. A few seconds later he reappeared with Darlene Trockworthy, their next-door neighbor. A peroxide blond with heavy blue eye-shadow, a too-tight dress and too-high heels, Darlene occasionally babysat Robbie and Sally. Darlene and Robbie were best friends, mainly because Darlene let Robbie eat as much dirt as he wanted, but between Darlene and Sally it had been war from the start.

Darlene slid into a seat at the kitchen table, aiming a kick at Melvin on the way. "Is that rat loose again?" she asked, her mouth full of the toast she had grabbed off of Robbie's plate.

Sally glared at her. "He's not a rat, you dingbat."

"Sally, watch your manners," Mr. Hesslop said sharply.

"Bill, the kid's rhyming again. I thought you said she'd grow out of that." Darlene pouted at Mr. Hesslop, her bright red lipstick spattered with toast crumbs. The whole neighborhood knew that Darlene had her "sights set" on Bill Hesslop, but so far he had resisted her advances.

"She'll grow out of it eventually," said Mr. Hesslop. "It's just a phase. Robbie, don't do that."

Robbie had climbed off his chair and was sitting on the floor, rubbing Cheerios in the dust on the floor before eating them.

Mr. Hesslop picked him up. "I'll clean up Mr. Dirt Devil here and drop him at his preschool. Can you take Sally?"

The look Darlene shot Sally clearly said that she'd like to dump Sally in San Francisco bay. Darlene sighed heavily. "Yeah, sure." She pointed a warning finger at Sally, a long red fingernail raking the air like a claw. "But no rhyming, kid. I mean it. One Iambic what-ya-ma-callit and I'm selling you to the slave traders. They'll ship you to Nebraska and make you shuck corn 'til you're eighty."

Sally smiled at her sweetly. "Your wish is my command. And your head is filled with sand." Sally scooped Melvin up, put him on her shoulder, and marched out of the kitchen.

"Put that rat back in his cage." Darlene yelled after her. "And if you're not ready in ten minutes I'm leaving without you."

Chapter Two

SALLY AND DARLENE maintained a careful no-touching distance as they headed down the hill to Sally's school. When a bike rider on the sidewalk forced them to shrink the gap between them they automatically sprang apart again after the bike had passed, as if repelled by a magnetic field.

Darlene examined her makeup in a compact mirror as she teetered along, causing oncoming pedestrians to grumble as they jumped out of her way. Sally practiced karate kicks, viciously attacking the most dangerous looking trash cans and mailboxes along their route, her backpack flopping wildly on her shoulders.

Halfway down the hill a posse of poodles suddenly rushed out the front door of a tall apartment building and made straight for Sally. Sally threw herself down on her knees and scooped up the scruffy little white poodle which was leading the pack. The little poodle yapped excitedly, licking Sally's face. The other three poodles were tall, black, and dignified, with the fur on their heads shaped into elegant topknots. They sniffed at Sally's backpack and at Darlene's shoes. One of them lifted his leg and took aim at Darlene's stiletto. Darlene shrieked and jumped back.

"Brutus! No!"

A chubby little girl about Sally's age ran up to them and grabbed the peeing poodle. She had black curly hair and large dark eyes. She was wearing a plaid skirt, a starched white blouse, and black patent leather shoes which looked extremely uncomfortable. "Brutus, you bad dog! Sorry, Miss Trockworthy. My Mom's trying to train him not to pee on everyone, but he forgets sometimes." She herded the poodles back up the front steps of the apartment building. "C'mon Brutus, Caesar, Nero, and Fluffy. You can't come to school with us. Poodles are not allowed. Go back upstairs."

Sally waved goodbye to Fluffy and stood up, dusting off her knees. "Hi, Katie! Are you ready to rumble?"

The chubby girl looked at her in confusion. "Huh?"

Sally skipped around Katie, chanting. "Charlie's a boy, so he's not too bright. We'll shout with joy when we win this fight."

Katie picked up the book bag she had dropped during the poodle roundup. A worried frown crinkled her pale forehead. "I don't know, Sally. Remember what happened the last time you got into a fight at school? Billy Lauder's tooth got knocked out and Arnold the Iguana ate it and had to go to the Pet Hospital. I don't want Arnold to go to the Pet Hospital. He doesn't like it there. Remember the time I put my Mom's Lilac Mist hand lotion on him because he looked dry? I thought it would make him feel better, but it turned him all pink and he had to go to the Pet Hospital so they could make him green again. Arnold hates being pink. Pink is a girl's color, and Arnold's a boy iguana. Mr. Zukas says so. So you shouldn't fight."

Katie looked ready to cry. Her large eyes grew red-rimmed and shiny. Sally patted her on the shoulder and handed her a wadded up Kleenex which she pulled out of her backpack. She resumed skipping in circles.

"Arnold's not going to the Pet Hospital this time," said Sally. "I have a new Secret Revenge Plan, and there aren't any iguanas in the plan."

Katie sniffed and wiped her nose. She followed Sally and Darlene as they continued down the hill. "Oh. Well, I guess it's okay then. I'm glad Arnold isn't in your new Secret Revenge Plan, cause iguanas don't like fighting."

They reached the bottom of the hill and turned onto a narrow side street lined with gingko trees. The sidewalk was covered with fan-shaped gingko leaves. Sally swooshed at them with the toes of her sneakers, sending the leaves swirling like tiny doves. Katie carefully stepped on the bare patches of sidewalk, keeping her shiny patent leather shoes free of leaf mush. Up ahead the street was jammed with cars disgorging kids with backpacks. The kids ran into the fenced-in playground of Montgomery Elementary School, a three-story brick building with sturdy granite columns flanking its front door. The building had a basketball court on one side and a cluster of crooked pine trees on the other side.

"Okay, you two," said Darlene, finally closing her compact. "Get lost. One of your parents will pick you up after school. Don't know which parent. Don't care." She sauntered off, popping a wad of gum into her mouth. Sally stuck her tongue out at Darlene's retreating back.

"You shouldn't do that," said Katie, gasping in horror. "My Mom says that kids should always show adults the proper respect."

Sally snorted. "Darlene's not an adult. She's a doofus." She skipped around Katie, chanting. "Darlene, Darlene, she's not too keen. She's the biggest dunce you've ever seen."

Katie turned red. She quickly looked around to make sure that Darlene hadn't heard. Darlene was examining her nails as she walked away, completely oblivious to the kids dodging around her on the sidewalk. Katie breathed a sigh of relief and followed Sally into the school building.

✦ ✦ ✦ ✦

"OKAY, EVERYONE SETTLE down!" Mr. Zukas' deep voice boomed

over the chaos in his fifth-grade classroom. He gave his sweater vest a firm tug and strode to the front of the class. "Get to your desks, pronto. Tommy, get your foot out of Kyle's mouth. Patricia, give Tiffany back her shoes. They're too small for you anyway, you clodhopper."

Thirty kids rushed to their seats with a sound like elephants tap dancing. Sally threw herself into her assigned seat in the front row of desks. Katie lowered herself demurely into the seat directly behind Sally. Arnold the Iguana calmly surveyed the classroom from his cage at the back.

Mr. Zukas opened a fat textbook. As he slowly searched for the page he wanted Sally started to fidget. She squirmed like an eel, sat on her hands, and finally couldn't contain herself any longer. She raised her arm and began waving it furiously back and forth. Mr. Zukas ignored her and turned another page.

Never one to be discouraged, Sally climbed onto her chair and waved both arms wildly like a pint-sized airport worker guiding a jumbo jet into a parking space.

"Sally Jane Hesslop," sighed Mr. Zukas, not looking up, "get down off of there before you break your neck. Not that I would mind, but the principal gets grumpy when students kick the bucket."

"Sorry, Mr. Zukas," said Sally, climbing down. "I just had a question. Can we have more discusses on evolution? Cause I looked it up on Google and a Google person says we came from tadpoles. I think it would be cool to be a tadpole. I had a tadpole once. I kept it in a Sprite bottle. After I drank the Sprite, of course. But then my brother Robbie drank the tadpole. Are we having fish sticks for lunch today?"

Mr. Zukas rubbed his forehead, looked longingly at the clock, and sighed again. "I haven't checked the lunch menu today, Sally. It's posted on the cafeteria door. You can check at recess. And no, we don't come from tadpoles. We are primates, which means we are related to the great apes. Our closest cousins are the chimpanzees. All of which I told you yesterday, and which you'd remember if you'd been paying attention. Now, class, open your history books to page thirty-four. The Pioneers. They crossed the Great Plains in covered wagons. Conditions were harsh. They had to hunt for their food."

A small red-haired boy wearing a shirt and tie waved politely from the desk next to Sally.

"Yes, Rodney?" asked Mr. Zukas. "Did you have a question?"

"Not a question, Mr. Zukas. Just a remark. It might interest the class to know that the Pioneers frequently ate deer as well as buffalo. They shot them with rifles."

Mr. Zukas beamed at him. "That's right, Rodney. I'm glad someone's been doing their homework."

Rodney smirked proudly while behind him the rest of the class rolled their eyes.

"Can anyone else tell me what other animals the Pioneers might have hunted?" asked Mr. Zukas.

Sally waved furiously.

"Anyone at all?" Mr. Zukas asked somewhat desperately.

Sally bounced up and down in her seat, arm still waving.

Mr. Zukas sighed. "Yes, Sally."

"They ate gophers."

Loud expressions of disgust erupted from the rest of the class. Sally turned around and glared at them.

"I'm fairly certain the Pioneers didn't eat gophers, Sally," said Mr. Zukas. "I believe gophers are inedible."

"Nuh-*uh,*" said Sally. "Gophers are super edible. The Pioneers roasted them over campfires and put hot sauce on them. They tasted like corn dogs. Only furry."

"Eeeww." The rest of the class unanimously decided it was grossed out. Rodney cleared his throat and looked disdainfully at Sally.

"In the unlikely event that the Pioneers ate gophers," said Rodney with a sneer, "they would have skinned them first. The fur would have been removed before roasting."

"Nuh-uh," retorted Sally. "The fur's where all the vitamins are. Just like potatoes. You keep the skin on for the vitamins."

Behind Sally, Katie gasped and put her hand over her mouth. She had turned a sickly shade of green.

Mr. Zukas peered at her. "Katie, do you need to use the Little Girl's Room?"

Katie nodded tearfully at him. He waved impatiently in the direction of the door and Katie dashed out of the classroom.

Mr. Zukas sighed and turned a page in his textbook. "Let's get off the topic of the Pioneers' diet. Class, have a look at the picture on the next page. See the tin star this man is wearing? That meant he was a sheriff. He kept order in the lawless Wild West. Of course, it was a difficult job, and he needed lots of help. Frequently he would deputize. That means to create a kind of temporary sheriff. Who do you think he deputized?"

"Hamsters," said Sally at once.

Mr. Zukas pulled at his tie, looking like he was tempted to strangle himself with it. "Hamsters cannot be deputies or anything else in the law enforcement arena, Sally. Hamsters are furry rodents, just like gophers."

Sally's eyes flashed dangerously. "Hamsters are nothing like gophers! Hamsters and gophers are sworn enemies. Just ask my hamster, Melvin. You don't want to get him started on gophers. He gets so mad his fur stands straight up and he hops around like microwave popcorn. Besides, hamsters can *so* be in the law enforcement arena. Melvin is in the law enforcement arena. He's a Secret Agent. He has a Secret Agent JetPack and everything. He straps it on and flies around San Francisco looking for bad guys. If he finds any bad guys he zaps them with his Secret Agent Laser Gun." Sally jumped up and aimed an imaginary laser gun at Mr. Zukas. "Kerpow!"

Mr. Zukas sighed and put a hand on his forehead. "Recess is early today," he said. "Everyone clear out of here. And stay out until the bell rings. I don't care if a tornado sweeps through the schoolyard. If anyone so much as puts one toe inside this classroom in the next half hour I'll personally feed them to the monster that lives in the school basement. He loves to snack on little kids. Especially ones who own hamsters."

✦ ✦ ✦ ✦

"THERE HE IS. Charlie Sanderson, Snot Extraordinaire. Are you ready?" Sally was on the Jungle Gym, hanging upside down by her knees. One of her braids had come undone and her long hair was covering her face. She parted it with her hands and peered at a blond-haired boy walking past. He was wearing baggy pants, expensive sneakers, and a backwards baseball cap and was surrounded by a bunch of boys dressed exactly like him.

Katie peered up at Sally worriedly from a safe perch on the lowest bar of the Jungle Gym. She had her skirt neatly tucked under her legs and her shiny patent leather shoes were carefully resting on a clean patch of grass. "Ready for what?" she asked.

"The Plan," whispered Sally.

"You never told me the plan. I don't know what to do. You just said you had a Secret Revenge Plan, and that there were no Iguanas."

"That's right," said Sally. "We don't need an Iguana for this plan, which is a good thing because Arnold the Iguana is retiring from the revenge business. Arnold had a little chat with Melvin at one of their Secret Agent meetings in the school cafeteria. Arnold told Melvin that he was getting too old for Secret Revenge Plans. He's going to retire to a home for elderly Iguanas in Florida. They spend all day sleeping in hammocks and drinking chocolate milkshakes. Melvin tried to talk him out of it. Mel's afraid Arnold will get fat from all the chocolate milkshakes, but Arnold's already pretty fat because Emily Niederbacher keeps feeding him her peanut butter and jelly sandwiches." Sally grabbed the Jungle Gym bar with both hands, flipped her legs through and dropped to the ground. "We don't need Arnold for this particular Secret Revenge Plan. You can be my back up. Follow me."

Katie sighed and reluctantly followed Sally across the playground.

Sally swerved around a group of kids playing hopscotch and sauntered in the direction of Charlie Sanderson and his posse, who were leaning against the schoolyard's chain-link fence and attempting to look cool. One of the boys nudged Charlie in the ribs and pointed at Sally.

Sally walked up to Charlie and slapped him on the back. "How's it going, Sanderson?"

The posse laughed and Charlie angrily pushed Sally away. "Get away from me, Hesslop, you freak."

Sally smiled. "I may be a freak, but you're a geek. And may I say, you really reek."

Charlie tried to shove her again, but Sally dodged away. She waved at Charlie as he and his posse stalked off to a far corner of the playground. Sally pulled something out of her pocket and tied it to the chain-link fence.

"What are you doing?" whispered Katie. "Are we going to get in trouble again? I can't go to the Principal's office again. I just can't. Mrs. Finsterman always says she's going to pinch my arm with that clothes pin she keeps on her desk."

"She won't pinch you," said Sally, watching the boys depart.

"How do you know? She always says she will."

"I know 'cause she always says she's going to pinch me too, but she never does. It's a psychotogical strategy, like when Xena pretended to be a goddess and the Mud People worshipped her."

Katie stared at her in bafflement. "Mrs. Finsterman is a Mud Person?"

Sally put a finger to her mouth to shush Katie and pointed at the group of boys. Charlie and his gang were about twenty yards away, torturing a first-grader by throwing pebbles at him. The first-grader hopped around like a frightened puppy, not sure whether to cry or run.

Sally checked the fence and muttered to herself. "Two more feet. Come on, you poophead. Keep walking."

Katie frowned at her in confusion. She peered at the group of boys then bent down to examine the fence. "Sally, what . . ."

Sally waved her arms to shush her. The school bell rang, signaling the end of recess. Kids started running for the doors. Charlie Sanderson and his posse followed at a leisurely pace. Suddenly Charlie halted, frowning. He pulled at the waistline of his baggy pants, shrugged, and took another step. Sally yanked Katie away from the fence, giggling wildly. She ran into the school building, pulling Katie along behind her.

A huge burst of laughter suddenly erupted from the school yard. Sally stood on her tiptoes and peeked out of the glass window in the front door of the building. Charlie Sanderson was standing in the middle of the playground with his baggy pants down around his ankles and his *Finding Nemo* underpants on display for all to see. Kids pointed at him, wetting themselves from laughing. Grinning wickedly, Sally pulled a small piece of fishing line from her pocket and showed it to Katie.

Chapter Three

SALLY WAS LYING on the floor of the Hesslop's living room, peering under an armchair. Muttering under her breath, she reached under the chair and pulled out a slinky and a blackened banana peel. Behind her, Robbie was sitting in the middle of the room wearing Snoopy underpants and his bike helmet. He giggled and whacked himself on the head with a toilet brush, matching the rhythm of Michael Jackson's *Beat it*, which was playing on the radio.

Sally sighed. The armchair was not delivering the goods. She crawled over to the sofa. Darlene Trockworthy was sitting there with her legs stretched out on the coffee table, painting her toenails. As she crawled under Darlene's legs Sally accidentally bumped them. A streak of Cotton Candy pink shot across Darlene's toes and up her ankle.

"Damn it, kid," groused Darlene, "Watch what you're doing. You made me mess up my pedicure."

"Sorry," Sally mumbled grudgingly. "It's just that I can't find Melvin. Have you seen him?"

"Nope, and good riddance," said Darlene. "That rodent's always creeping around underfoot. I swear he tries to trip me on purpose."

Sally sat back on her heels and smirked at Darlene. "He does that 'cause it's part of his Secret Mission. He's Special Agent Melvin, and he goes to Washington BC every weekend for Super Secret Hamster Orders. He's trained to trip all enemy combatants."

Darlene wiped the nail polish off her foot. "Well, if you can't find him maybe he's at the White House meeting the President," she said. "I hear they serve hamster every Friday."

Sally gave her an evil glare and flopped on her stomach to peer under the sofa.

Behind her Melvin suddenly appeared, rolling across the living room on an old-fashioned four-wheeled roller skate. His chubby rear-end didn't quite fit on the skate, and he dusted a path across the floor with his fur. He rolled from one end of the room to the other and disappeared into the kitchen. Robbie waved the toilet brush at him as he passed.

Sally pulled her head out from under the sofa and hopped to her feet. She planted her fists on her hips. "Drat you, Melvin. Where *are* you? If you're hiding in the microwave again I'm going to spank your little furry butt. You know Dad hates it when his microwave popcorn tastes like hamster."

She stomped into the kitchen and opened the microwave. No Melvin. She banged open cupboards and rattled pans. "Melvin, if you've gone on a Secret Mission again you are soooo in trouble. You know you aren't supposed to go on Secret Missions after your bedtime. I'm gonna write to Washington. They'll remote you back to Janitor Melvin and take away your Secret Agent Jetpack."

Sally crawled under the kitchen table and peered inside an empty box of Wheaties. Behind her Melvin had managed (by methods known only to himself and other Secret Agent Hamsters) to get himself on top of the fridge. He poked his nose over the side and surveyed the perilous drop to the kitchen counter. After a moment's hesitation, he stepped off the fridge, executing a perfect swan dive with a half-twist. He landed face-first on the kitchen counter then slowly toppled over onto his back, legs in the air. He tried to roll onto his feet but was hampered by a touch of middle-aged spread. After several tries he got himself right-side up and waddled to the edge of the countertop. At that moment Robbie wandered in, fencing with his toilet brush. Melvin took a step into the unknown and landed splat on top of Robbie's bike helmet, all four feet splayed out and hanging on for dear life. Oblivious to his stowaway, Robbie fenced back into the living room, taking Melvin with him.

"Sally, get off the floor," said Mr. Hesslop as he entered the kitchen, a pencil behind his ear and the grumpy look of a man who's just been wrestling with his tax returns. "You're as bad as Robbie. Remember, you're supposed to set a good example for him. Now, go brush your teeth. It's bedtime."

Sally scrambled out from under the table and saluted. "Sir. Yes Sir. Your orders we obey. We're here to save the day. Good dental hygiene is a must. We'll clean our teeth or bust." She marched out of the kitchen, humming a martial tune. At the end of the hall she pivoted sharply and entered a small bathroom whose plumbing fixtures dated from the fifties. A bulging hamper full of wet towels sat in the corner and a flotilla of rubber ducks was lined up along the edge of the bathtub. The back of the toilet overflowed with half-empty shampoo bottles.

Sally knelt and began throwing towels out of the hamper. "Melvin, you varmint, you're about to become a garment. My Xena doll needs a fur coat, and you've got my vote."

She stuck her head into the now empty hamper. Behind her Melvin sauntered into the bathroom and scrambled up onto the edge of the tub, climbing the pyramid of wet towels Sally had dumped on the floor. He wound his way along the rim of the bathtub, which was full of soapy water leftover from Robbie's bath. Melvin dodged the rubber ducks with surprising agility, but overconfidence got the better of him and he slipped, falling into the bathtub with a splash.

Sally pulled her head out of the hamper and rushed over. "Melvin, you poophead. Your Secret Agent Swimming Lessons aren't til next week."

A stream of bubbles floating up from under the water was the only answer. Sally scooped Melvin up and deposited him on the bathroom rug. Melvin shook like a tiny dog and sat shivering, his orange fur matted to his sides.

"It's okay, Mel," said Sally. "I'll fix you right up with my Top Secret Air Blaster."

She grabbed a blow drier and turned it on High. The blast of hot air rolled Melvin over backward. He did a full somersault and ended up on standing on his head against the side of the bathtub. Sally picked him up and aimed the blow drier at his tummy. His fur blew straight backward as if he was in a hurricane. When Sally had finished drying him he was twice his normal size and had the hamster version of an Afro.

"Melvin! That's a great disguise. You can use it on your next undercover mission. Nobody will ever recognize you. You can be Horace the Hairdresser, famous for your skills with a curling iron. All the lady hamsters will be lining up to make an appointment with you."

Melvin's Afro started to deflate.

"Hang on Melvin," said Sally. "You just need some Product to maintain volume. That's what those hair commercials on TV are always saying."

Sally grabbed a can of hair mousse from the cabinet under the sink and sprayed a big glob on Melvin, who promptly disappeared under a pile of foam. Sally dug him out of the foam and rubbed the mousse into his fur, then snatched a toothbrush from the sink. "This is Dad's. He won't mind," said Sally as she brushed Melvin's fur into spikes. She sat him back down on the bathroom rug.

"There! You totally look like a cool dude. You look like one of those singers on American Idol. You just need to learn how to dance."

Sally jumped up and launched into a wild dance step. Melvin backed into a corner as Sally's flailing arms whacked the shower curtain and knocked a shampoo bottle into the toilet. Sally finished with a flourish and bowed low before an imaginary audience. "C'mon Mel. It's not hard. You just do little wiggle and a little rap. You just gotta have attitude. Like this."

Sally grabbed a rubber duck and sang into it like a microphone. "My name's Sally J. and I'm here to say, I'm doing my dance 'cause I pulled down Charlie's pants."

Sally picked up Melvin and danced around with him. "You need a hamster rap. All the tough hamsters have one. And maybe some bling. I wonder if Dad would buy you a gold chain."

Melvin looked decidedly skeptical about this, not to mention seasick from all the dancing.

Sally danced into her bedroom, singing. "I'm furry and I'm cute. I'm a Secret Agent to boot. I've got a special JetPack which is totally wack."

She tucked Melvin into his Hamster Habitat. Melvin trundled down the orange tube to his usual nest, his sticky moussed fur attracting bits of sawdust. By the time he reached his nest in the middle of the Habitat he looked like a tiny pile of kindling.

"Another super disguise, Mel," said Sally. "Totally cool. You can do your next Secret Mission at Tony's Pizza. They have sawdust all over their floor. They'll never spot you. You can sneak into the kitchen and find out the ingredients of their Secret Pizza Sauce."

Melvin burrowed into the sawdust of his nest until he was just a sawdust-lump. Sally yawned and blew him a kiss. "Night Mel."

Chapter Four

"SALLY JANE HESSLOP, you are a demon spawn."

Mrs. Patterson, leader of Brownie Troop 112, wiped the milk off her sour face and glared down at Sally. The two of them were faced off in the middle of the Montgomery Elementary School cafeteria. A table with cartons of milk and a plate of Rice Krispie Treats was setup in one corner.

The wayward milk had ended up on Mrs. Patterson's face through totally unavoidable circumstances. Sally had been chasing another Brownie while holding a carton of milk and a straw. Squirting had been inevitable.

Sally planted her fists on her hips and regaled Mrs. Patterson with a cold stare. They were old enemies. They had disliked each other from the very first day that Mrs. Patterson had assumed the leadership of the troop. On that fateful day Sally had been showing the other brownies how to slide along the newly polished wooden floor in their stocking feet. She had just launched into a particularly energetic slide when Mrs. Patterson had walked through the door of the cafeteria. The resulting collision had knocked Mrs. Patterson off her feet and onto her support-hose covered knees. Mrs. Patterson had been trying to transfer Sally to another Brownie troop ever since, so far without success.

"Well," said Sally, "if I'm a demon spawn then I bet it's a cool demon, one that can shoot flames out of its eyeballs. I wish I could shoot flames out of my eyeballs. I'd turn Charlie Sanderson into a crispy critter."

Mrs. Patterson raised her eyes to the heavens. "When I say that you are a demon spawn, Sally Jane Hesslop, it means that you are a very bad girl. One of the worst I've had the misfortune to meet in all my years of guiding Brownies along the difficult path to becoming young ladies."

Sally fiddled with her straw. "I'd rather be a demon spawn than a young lady. I bet demon spawn have cool super powers. The coolest super power would be to turn people into potato bugs. My first victim would be Charlie Sanderson. If I turned him into a potato bug it would be a big improvement. I'd probably get a medal from the President. Then they'd have a parade for me and I'd ride on a float past the White House and wave to the crowd. Like this." Sally energetically waved her arms, spraying drops of milk onto Mrs. Patterson's bouffant hairdo.

Mrs. Patterson closed her eyes and kneaded her forehead with two shaking fingers. "Sally Jane Hesslop, we were discussing you spewing milk everywhere and making a mess, not super powers and potato bugs. Now go get some paper towels from the restroom and wipe this up."

"Okay" said Sally, shrugging. She tucked the straw under her Brownie beanie. "When do we get to make bird feeders from pinecones? That's in the Brownie handbook, you know. Page forty-nine. You stick peanut butter in the pinecones so the birds can peck it out. Though I don't understand why we can't just spread the peanut butter on Ritz crackers. Then the birds could peck it real easy. Molly Sanderson says it's because the birds like to work hard for their food, but that's just stupid. Besides, Molly is Charlie Sanderson's sister and she picks her nose, so you know anything she says is suspected. That's what my Dad says. Nose pickers are Dim Bulbs and to be suspected. The crackers don't have to be Ritz. Wheat Thins would work good too."

Mrs. Patterson sighed. "Sally Jane Hesslop, I don't know what you're blathering on about. Get this mess cleaned up. *Now.*"

Mindy Nichols, a thin black girl with red bows on the ends of her cornrows, ran up to Sally. She peered after the departing Mrs. Patterson with a fearful expression. "Sally, guess what? Mrs. Osterman isn't coming today. She's in the hospital."

Mrs. Osterman was the co-leader of the troop. She was a quiet young woman with a warm smile who was liked by all the Brownies.

"You mean it's just us and Prissy Patterson?" groaned Sally. "Oh barf. Why is Mrs. Osterman in the hospital?"

"Molly Sanderson says it's because she's having an *operation,*" whispered Mindy.

Sally rolled her eyes. "Molly is always saying stupid stuff. You know that. She's a Sanderson. You can't believe anything she says. C'mon. Let's go ask Sandra Chang. She'll know."

Sally and Mindy ran up to a group of girls gathered around Sandra Chang, a tall, graceful Chinese girl with a curtain of shiny black hair hanging all the way to her hips. A purple silk scarf was artfully tied around the neck of her Brownie uniform.

Sally barged her way through the group. "Hey Sandra."

Sandra nodded at her graciously, like a benevolent Queen acknowledging her subjects.

"Sandra, what's up with Mrs. Osterman? Mindy says she's in the hospital."

"I'm sorry, Sally," replied Sandra Chang in a quiet, authoritative voice. "I don't know the details. All I know is that Mrs. Patterson is taking over as Troop Leader."

Loud groans erupted from all the Brownies within earshot. Molly Sanderson, a short, pudgy blond girl with two front teeth missing, sister to the infamous Charlie Sanderson, jumped up and down frantically, waving her hand as if in school.

"Thandra. Thandra," lisped Molly, "I know what'th happened to Mrs. Othterman. My brother Charlie told me."

On hearing Charlie's name Sally made loud gagging noises and clutched her throat. Molly ignored her, looking intently at Sandra. Finally Sandra gave her a regal nod.

"Mrs. Othterman ith having a Hystertology," whispered Molly excitedly. "That'th an operation. It meanth thee can't have babiesth anymore, unlesth she goeth to Mexico and getsth it reverthed. Then her babiesth will come out backwardsth, like when your Dad backth the car out of the garage. Latht week my Dad backed our car out of the garage and ran over my brother'th bicycle. My Dad said a very bad wordth."

Sally planted her hands on her hips and gave Molly a look of scathing contempt. "That's not a Hystertology, Sanderson. A Hystertology is when you have your ears pinned back. The doctor staples them to your head so you don't look like Dumbo."

"Mrs. Othterman doesthn't look like Dumbo," said Molly.

"Well, not anymore," shot back Sally. "She's had a Hystertology. Sheesh, Sanderson. You are such a dimwit sometimes. I guess it runs in the family."

Molly advanced on her, fists clenched. "You take that back Hessthlop."

Sally assumed a Xena fighting pose. "C'mon, Sanderson. I'll lick you, and then I'll go lick your stupid brother."

"Charlie's a twit,
He's Molly's brother.
He has half a wit,
Molly has the other."

Sally raised her leg in preparation for a super-duper martial arts kick. Molly stood her ground for a second, then thought better of it and dashed off to find Mrs. Patterson.

"Girls! Girls!" shouted Mrs. Patterson from the center of the cafeteria. "Everyone gather round. It's Share Time. Bring the item you're going to share with the group over here."

There was a noisy scramble as all the Brownies rushed to a pile of backpacks stacked against the wall, and then convened in the center of the room. They threw themselves on the wooden floor in a cross-legged circle around Mrs. Patterson.

"Molly, dear, why don't you go first," said Mrs. Patterson.

Molly Sanderson smirked at the others and walked to the center of the circle. She held up a Barbie doll dressed in an immaculate princess-type costume of white silk with a red velvet cape. "Thith ith Princeth Thophie of Bavaria. Thee's dressthed for the ball. Thee's a Spethial Edition. My Mom bought her for me in New York at Bloomingdaleth."

"She's just beautiful, Molly," said Mrs. Patterson. "So precious. I bet all the young ladies here want to be Princesses, don't you, girls?"

Sally sprang up. "Of course. I'm Princess Scary Fighting Eagle from the Moping Moose tribe. We get dressed for balls too. We paint our faces with red stripes, stick eagle feathers in our ears, and do our Special Moose Waltz around the campfire."

Sally launched into a fast-paced dance, shaking her arms and kicking her legs over her head. Her Brownie beanie flew off, and girls scrambled backwards as she lunged wildly toward them. She concluded by spinning rapidly in a circle, then staggered dizzily back to her spot on the floor.

Mrs. Patterson closed her eyes during this performance. After Sally had sat down again she opened her eyes, a pained expression on her face. "Mindy," she sighed, "why don't you go next?"

Mindy Nichols moved to the center of the circle, bashfully pulling at her cornrows. She pulled a brightly colored paper bird from a bag. Several of the Brownies oohed and aahed. Mindy smiled gratefully. "This is a Japanese art called Origami. My Mom learned it when she was stationed at a Navy base in Sasebo, Japan. She taught it to me. This is a tsuru. That's Japanese for crane. All the kids in Japan learn to make them. The crane is a symbol of peace." Mindy sat down abruptly, looking embarrassed. The Brownies applauded.

Mrs. Patterson pursed her lips as if she'd just drunk lemon juice. "Very, er, multi-cultural, Mindy. Though maybe you should bring something a little more American next time. These exotic things aren't really Brownie appropriate for Brownie meetings. Let's see, Sandra, why don't you come up."

Sandra Chang nodded and rose gracefully to her feet. She unrolled a paper scroll which displayed a vertical line of beautiful Chinese characters. "This is called calligraphy. It's a very popular art in China. These characters are in the Mandarin language, which my mother and grandmother speak. My grandmother taught me how to do calligraphy. We use a pot of black ink and a brush made of sheep's hair."

Sandra sat down and the Brownies applauded respectfully.

"My goodness," said Mrs. Patterson, "This is certainly an international group. I feel like I'm at the United Nations. Well, onward. Who'd like to volunteer?"

Sally waved her arm wildly. Another Brownie across from Sally dared to raise her arm as well. Sally glared daggers at her opponent, and the offending Brownie promptly dropped her challenge and looked like she'd be thrilled to sink into the floor. Mrs. Patterson tried mightily to avoid Sally's gaze, but resistance was futile. Sally marched unbidden to the center of the circle, carrying a paper takeout carton. Mrs. Patterson raised her eyes heavenward.

"I'll go next, Mrs. Patterson," said Sally. She opened the carton and pulled out something wriggly. The Brownies gasped in horror and the ones closest scooted away. Molly Sanderson screamed.

"Mrsth. Patterthon, Thally'th brought a rat! Eeeuww. Make her take ith away!"

Sally rolled her eyes. "It's not a rat, Sanderson, you doofus. It's my hamster, Melvin. My Dad shaved him. See, what happened was, I put some of Darlene Trockworthy's Super Hold Hair Mousse on him. Darlene wants to be my Dad's girlfriend, and she left her hair mousse in our bathroom."

Mrs. Patterson clutched the pearls around her neck and muttered something about tramps.

"Anyway," continued Sally, "it turns out you should never mousse a hamster. It glues their fur up something awful. Plus you should especially never put mousse on your hamster and then let him roll around in sawdust. My Dad said there must have been some kind of chemical reaction between the pine sap in the sawdust and Darlene's Super Hold Hair Mousse. It hardened up like that shellac stuff we used on our birdhouses last year. Poor Mel here couldn't even walk. He just rolled around like a pinecone with feet. So my Dad used his electric razor and shaved off all of Melvin's fur. So now Mel's got a crew cut, like an Army guy. Anybody want to hold him?"

The Brownies all recoiled. Melvin dove back into the takeout container as Mrs. Patterson stepped forward and made shooing motions at Sally. Sally reluctantly relinquished center stage and sat back down. She dropped a Rice Krispie Treat into the takeout carton. "It's okay, Mel," she whispered into the carton, "Don't mind Prissy Patterson. The troop loved you. You were a big hit."

Chapter Five

"I WISH YOU could have been there, Katie. Melvin was the star of the show. It was like American Idol, but with hamsters."

Sally and Katie were walking across a wide green lawn. Sally was wearing baggy blue shorts and a T-shirt that said "Girl Power!" in sparkly red and blue letters. On her feet she had one red basketball sneaker and one black one. Katie was uncomfortably over-dressed, as usual, in a starched white blouse with a Peter Pan collar, a kilt, and black patent-leather Mary Janes. Sally was swinging a takeout container by its wire handle.

"American what?" asked Katie.

"Oh jeez Katie. Are your parents *ever* going to let you watch TV?"

"Probably not. They say it turns your brain into Swiss Cheese."

"That's just stupid," said Sally. "Everyone knows that brains are made out of spaghetti. Don't you remember Mindy's Halloween party? We had to put our hands in the brains, and they were spaghetti. Cooked spaghetti, of course. Nobody has raw spaghetti for brains, except maybe Charlie Sanderson. Hey, want to see Melvin's outfit?"

She stopped and set the takeout container down on the grass. When she opened it Melvin popped his head out, his whiskers twitching. He was wearing a purple and white striped doggie sweater. Sally picked him up and held him out to Katie, who scratched his shaved head. Melvin yawned and had a good stretch, waving his tiny tail back and forth, which was the only part of him which still had fur on it. Sally put him on her shoulder. "Isn't this sweater cute? Mel was cold without his fur, so my Dad bought it at a pet store. They didn't have any hamster sweaters, so he got this one. It's for Chihuahua puppies. Melvin didn't want to wear kid's clothes, but I finally talked him into it."

"It's very stylish," said Katie.

"You bet," said Sally, scratching Melvin's nose. "Mel's a stylin' dude. I wish you could have been at our Brownie meeting. We had Show and Tell. Sandra Chang brought some fancy writing called colonoscopy, cause she's Chinese. Mindy Nichols brought this paper bird called a guru. You could have brought that droodle toy. I don't get why your parents hate the Brownies."

"It's a dreidel, not a droodle. And my parents don't hate the Brownies. They just don't like Mrs. Patterson. They don't like the way she's always telling people they aren't American."

"Yeah, she's stuck on that," said Sally. "My Dad says she's got a psychotological problem about it. A Pixation. That's when Pixies get inside your head and turn your brain into scrambled eggs. Hey, if Mrs. Patterson watches a lot of TV and your parents are right about the Swiss Cheese, then her brain will turn into a cheese omelet."

They passed through a garden full of pink and yellow roses. In front of them loomed an imposing mansion flanked by towering oak trees. A driveway bordered with rhododendrons led to the front entrance, but Sally headed toward a door on the side of the house.

Katie glanced around nervously. "Gosh, this is a very fancy house. Is your grandma nice?" she asked, her voice shaking.

"Oh yeah," said Sally. "She's super nice. Well, to me, anyway. She's only mean to people she doesn't like. Like salespeople and missionaries. She chases them. Once she chased this missionary all the way down the driveway. She was hitting him on the head with a broom. She said she wanted to hit him on the head with a shovel, but then she'd have to hide the body. Bodies are hard to hide. They turn into zombies and start showing up every day for breakfast. And my grandma *hates* having guests for breakfast. She always has her breakfast in bed. A piece of toast with two poached eggs and her special coffee. I tasted her special coffee once. It made me hiccup. My Dad took it away and said I was too young for special coffee."

Katie started to whimper quietly. "What if she doesn't like *me*?"

Sally patted her on the shoulder. "Don't worry, Katie. I promise she'll like you. It's just salespeople, missionaries, and Mean Darlene Trockworthy she doesn't like. Grandma says Darlene is on the make. That means she wears too much makeup. Which is *sooo* true. Once I saw a huge piece of her face fall off. It just peeled off like a big piece of paint peeling off a wall. It was *so* gross."

Katie turned a bit green around the gills. She took an embroidered handkerchief out of the pocket of her kilt and coughed into it. Sally went up to the side of the house and stood on tiptoe to peer in a window. Robbie was inside the house. All that could be seen of him was his rear-end, which was hanging over the edge of a large pot full of daisies. Sally pushed open the side door.

"C'mon, Katie," said Sally. "It'll be fine, you'll see."

Sally skipped into the room and grabbed hold of Robbie's shorts, hauling him out of the flowerpot. Robbie was wearing a little sailor suit and tennis shoes. A goatee of dirt circled his mouth. Sally sighed and shook her head. Robbie grinned at her and held up a worm in his chubby little fist. Sally grabbed it a split second before he put it in his mouth. She deposited the worm back into the flowerpot.

"Katie, can I borrow your handkerchief?"

Katie looked at her, then down at Robbie. She reluctantly pulled out her lacy handkerchief and handed it over. Sally scrubbed Robbie's face with it until his face turned red and the handkerchief turned brown. Robbie giggled and ran off, pulling another worm out of the pocket of his sailor suit.

"C'mon," said Sally. "Just follow Robbie. He's probably headed straight for grandma. She always stuffs him with sugar cookies. They're his favorite. After dirt, of course. And dust bunnies. He's been on a dust bunny binge lately. Yesterday my Dad found him under his bed, rolling the dust bunnies into little pancakes and pouring maple syrup on them."

Sally and Katie ran after Robbie, who led them down a hallway lined with beautiful silk wallpaper. Robbie ran his hand along the wallpaper, leaving a long brown streak of dirt. At the end of the hall he darted out of a sliding glass door.

When Sally and Katie followed Robbie through the door they found themselves on a patio which had a spectacular view of San Francisco bay and the Golden Gate Bridge.

Bill Hesslop, dressed in a suit and tie, was perched on the edge of a deckchair. Next to him, stretched out comfortably on a matching chair, was Sally's grandmother. Mrs. Belinda Worthington was a trim, stylish woman of sixty-five with white hair and blue eyes. She wore tailored trousers and a cashmere sweater. Robbie ran up to her, pulling something out of the pocket of his sailor suit.

Mrs. Worthington held out her hand. "What have you got there, Mr. Robert?"

Robbie deposited a large pink earthworm into her hand. Bill Hesslop winced, but Mrs. Worthington didn't even blink. "Well. This is a fine big wriggler, isn't he? It's too bad your grandpa isn't with us anymore. He'd take this fine specimen down to the pond and show you how to catch a fish with him. The gardener stocks the pond with trout, you know."

Robbie nodded at her solemnly. "Fishes eat worms." Robbie took the worm back and tried to put it in his mouth, but his grandmother was too quick for him. She calmly snatched up the worm and handed it to Bill Hesslop. "Bill, dear. Dispose of this, would you."

"Yes, ma'am." He sighed and carried the worm down to the lawn. Sally ran up to Mrs. Worthington and gave her a hug. "Hi, grandma! Look who I brought! This is my best friend, Katie Greenwald. Just so you know, Katie's not a salesperson or a missionary. She's a fifth-grader. We're in the same class at school."

Sally waved at Katie to come nearer, but Katie shook her head vigorously, looking terrified.

Mrs. Worthington smiled at her. She picked up a plate of cookies from a small table next to her deckchair. "Katie, I can tell by your tasteful outfit that you are a young lady of distinction. Now, I have here some wonderfully refined Petit Fours which I'm sure will appeal to your palate. Come try one."

Katie shyly approached and took a cookie. "It's very nice, ma'am."

"Such lovely manners," said Mrs. Worthington. "You could learn a thing or two from your friend, Miss Sally."

Sally tried to swallow the cookie she'd grabbed and stuffed into her mouth. "I have super good manners," she said, her voice muffled by cookie. "You told me so last time I was here, grandma. You said my compartments were spotless."

"Your comportment, dear. Your comportment was spotless. It means you were behaving like a little lady during that visit. Quite out of character, it was. You must have been ill. Perhaps a touch of flu. Usually you dash about like a little wombat that's gotten into my diet pills."

"What's a wombat?" asked Sally, taking another cookie.

"A small creature, dear. Very hyperactive. Speaking of small creatures, where is that animal you're always carting around? I hope he isn't loose in the house. Last time you were here Cook found him in the pantry. He popped out at her from behind a jar of pickled beets. She came running to me, screaming something about mice and threatening to quit. It took a bottle of my best brandy to calm her down."

"Melvin's right here, grandma. See?" Sally pointed at her shoulder, but Melvin wasn't there. Sally lifted her hair and felt around the back of her neck. No Melvin.

Her grandmother gave her a suspicious look. "Sally Jane Hesslop. Is that miniature marauder loose in my house again?"

"No, no," said Sally hurriedly. "Everything's fine, grandma. I put Melvin in a safe place, where he wouldn't bother anybody. I'll just go check on him." She made shooing motions at Katie, who backed nervously towards the house. Sally walked nonchalantly to the door, then yanked it open and pushed Katie through.

"Dang that Melvin," Sally grouched as she dashed down the hall. "He must have jumped ship and gone exploring. C'mon, Katie. We have to find him before Mrs. Beatty does. That's grandma's cook. She makes the best fudge brownies in the world, and grandma's always saying she loves Mrs. Beatty's cooking better than she loves her own family. Grandma'll be really mad if Mrs. Beatty leaves on account of Melvin."

Katie puffed along behind Sally. "Why does Mrs. Beatty hate Melvin?" she asked breathlessly. "He's a nice hamster. Even my Mom likes him. Remember that time you brought him over to our apartment? My Mom said he was a prince among gerbils."

"Well, of course he's a prince among gerbils," said Sally. "Hamsters are way, way better than stinky old gerbils. Mrs. Beatty's problem is she can't tell that Melvin's a hamster. She thinks he's a mouse. Every time she sees him she tries to hit him with her rolling pin."

Katie gasped in horror.

Sally sang a tune as she ran:

"Mel, I know you're in the house.
Mrs. Beatty thinks you're a mouse.

Come out before you get bashed.
Hamsters look better un-smashed."

Suddenly a loud scream echoed through the house. "Shoot!" said Sally. "That's Mrs. Beatty. C'mon!"

They rushed into the kitchen, where Mrs. Beatty was standing near the oven wearing her usual uniform of flower-print dress, hairnet, and apron. Interrupted in the middle of her daily baking, she was eyeing a mixing bowl and waving a rolling pin at it. She took a step towards the bowl as it rattled. Whiskers poked over the edge, then slid back down. When they appeared again, the flour-covered head of Melvin could be seen peering over the edge of the bowl.

Melvin squirmed and wriggled and managed to pull himself up onto the rim of the bowl. It tottered and tipped over, spilling Melvin and a cascade of flour onto the kitchen counter.

Mrs. Beatty let out a war whoop and brought the rolling pin crashing down onto the counter. She missed Melvin by a whisker. He scrambled along the flour-dusted countertop, dashed around a carton of eggs, and dove head first into the open maw of a food processor. Mrs. Beatty yelled in triumph and leapt forward. She hit the 'On' switch of the food processor.

The processor began to spin, taking Melvin with it. He went around, faster and faster. Just as he was in danger of becoming hamster McNuggets he was flung out of the food processor. He flew through the air and landed face first in a bowl full of walnuts, scattering nuts everywhere.

The walnuts shifted under his feet as Melvin frantically sped up, trying to scramble out of the bowl. Nuts started flying through the air like tiny cannonballs, pelting Mrs. Beatty in the face. She raised her rolling pin and warded them off like a Jedi master blocking bullets with his light saber.

Mrs. Beatty hit a walnut through the open kitchen window, clobbering a pigeon which was flying across the lawn. It squawked and crash-landed on the grass. Ducking walnuts, Sally grabbed Melvin and jumped back out of range of Mrs. Beatty's rolling pin. Melvin shook himself, showering Sally in flour. "Jeez, Mel," said Sally. "What a mess. You need a bath. You look like a dumpling with feet."

"A bath!" yelled Mrs. Beatty, shaking her rolling pin. "Do not talk to me of baths! What is needed is a mousetrap with a nice strong spring. Snap!" She whacked her rolling pin down on the counter with a bang.

Sally and Katie jumped. "C'mon, Mrs. Beatty," said Sally. "You don't really mean that. Melvin's very sorry he disturbed your cooking. Aren't you, Mel?" Sally held Melvin up to her eyes and glared at him.

Melvin stared back at her and yawned. He was clearly not in an apologetic mood, rolling pin or no rolling pin.

Mrs. Beatty snorted and shook the rolling pin at them. "Out of my kitchen! All of you! I am making croque en bouche. It is a very delicate process, not to be interrupted by small children and mice! Out!"

Sally, Katie, and Melvin beat a hasty retreat.

✦ ✦ ✦ ✦

"I BET THEY'VE gone down to the stables," said Sally, surveying the empty patio. Her father, grandmother, and Robbie were nowhere to be seen. A lone sparrow pecked at the crumbs of the Petit Fours. "C'mon, maybe grandma'll let us ride Max!" She dashed down the steps of the patio two at a time and headed across the lawn.

"Who's Max?" Katie asked, breath coming in gasps as she tried to keep up.

"He's a Shetland pony," said Sally, slowing down so Katie could catch up. "He's super gentle. You can ride on his back without a saddle. Plus he's got long blond hair called a mane. Grandma lets me brush it. When it's brushed Max looks just like a princess. Well, he would if he weren't a horse. Or a boy."

"I don't know if I want to meet Max," Katie said dubiously. "I think I might be afraid of horses."

"What do you mean, 'might' be? Don't you know?"

"I'm not sure," said Katie. "I've never seen a horse, not in person I mean."

Sally changed course and headed for a birdbath in the center of the lawn. "You have *so* seen a horse. Remember that policeman who yelled at us just cause we were climbing that lamppost? He was riding a horse."

"He was yelling at *you*, not me," said Katie. "*I* wasn't climbing the lamppost. I was holding your backpack and Melvin. Melvin didn't want to climb the lamppost either. And the horse was way over across the street. If the horse had been on our side of the street I'm pretty sure I would have been afraid of it."

"Well, you won't be afraid of Max. And anyway, he's a pony, not a horse. Ponies are kinda like horses that have shrunk. You know, like that time my Dad wasn't home and I did the laundry all by myself and all of my Dad's sweaters shrank. It was weird. They came out of the dryer looking like little kids clothes. Robbie wears them now. Your Mom's got some nice sweaters. I specially like that pink fuzzy one. If you ever want some new clothes, just do the laundry." Sally stopped at the birdbath. It had moss growing along its sides and was full of rainwater. A sparrow was perched on the rim, watching them warily. "Okay, Mel. It's bath time."

She lowered Melvin into the water. When she let go he promptly sank down to the moldy bottom of the birdbath. Sally grabbed him off the bottom and swished him around in the water, leaving a trail of flour floating like dust on the water's surface.

"There you go, Mel. Much better. Though I can see you're overdue for your Secret Agent swimming lessons. You might want to sign up next time you're in Washington BC. And make sure you use Water

Wings the first time. Katie uses them."

"Oh, yes", said Katie, nodding enthusiastically. "Definitely use Water Wings, Melvin. One time, Charlie Sanderson pushed me into the pool at Rimrock Park when I wasn't wearing my Water Wings. The lifeguard had to pull me out and hit my back to get all the water out. I had pool water in my tummy for days afterward. You could hear it splashing around when I walked."

Melvin regarded her with appropriate solemnity upon hearing this information.

Sally pulled off Melvin's wet sweater and set him on her shoulder. "I hope he doesn't catch cold. Melvin's very delicate. And sensitive. My Dad says he's an old soul. That means he's a good listener. He knows all kinds of super-secret stuff, but he never tells anyone. That would be against the Super Secret Hamster Code of Rules and Regulations. Nope, if you've got a secret, tell a hamster."

"Gerbils are verbal
And sip tea that is herbal.
They gossip and chat
About this and that.
So if you've got secrets to tell,
A hamster is swell.
Do what you will,
They'll never spill."

Sally and Katie (and Melvin, shivering on Sally's shoulder and dripping water down the back of her t-shirt) followed a stone-covered path which led from the lawn into a grove of birch trees. A patch of bluebells clustered under the waving trees. Sally picked one of the tiny flowers and held it up for Melvin to sniff. He nosed it warily and then suddenly swallowed it, causing hamster convulsions as he choked on the petals. To prevent himself from falling off Sally's shoulder Melvin dug his claws into her T-shirt.

"Ouch! Dang it Melvin, that hurt." Sally detached him from her T-shirt and held him up at eye level. "What do you say? Hmm?"

Melvin was not known for his expressiveness, but it did appear that his whiskers had a hint of apology about them.

"That's right," said Sally. "You say you're sorry. Grandma's always saying how I need some etiquette lessons. Maybe you should have some too. You can't be a Secret Agent if you don't have good etiquette."

"What's etiquette?" asked Katie.

"It's these rules on how to behave in all situations. Like, if you burp really loudly at a fancy dinner party you should point to the person next to you. Hamsters know all these rules automatically, but I think maybe Melvin needs a refresher course."

Up ahead the trees thinned out and the path they were on ended at a white-fenced corral. Mrs. Worthington was mounted on a chestnut mare, putting the glossy-coated horse through its paces. Together horse and rider turned and spun expertly around the corral. Mrs. Worthington sat with her back straight as a ruler. They picked up speed and sailed over a jump made of red and white striped poles, the horse's hooves clearing the top pole with ease. Bill Hesslop and Robbie clapped from their seats on a pile of hay bales.

"Wow! Look at your grandmother!" said Katie as they climbed onto the fence of the corral to watch. "How come she doesn't fall off?"

"Oh, she practices all the time." said Sally. "Grandma says she started riding when she was two. Her Dad put her on a pony and then gave it a spanking. It took off and ran right through some rose bushes and then up those steps in the backyard and into the house. My Dad says grandma is exaggerating about the 'into the house' part. He says I get my linguistic flexibility from her. That means I can roll my tongue into funny shapes." Sally stuck her tongue out at Katie and rolled it into a "U" shape.

Katie looked impressed and tried to roll her tongue too, but couldn't quite manage it. She pushed at it with her fingers, but finally gave up. "Your grandmother must be very rich, to live in this big house and have horses and everything. How come you and your Dad and Robbie live in such a small apartment?"

"It's because of the prostate," said Sally, laying Melvin's wet sweater on the top rail of the fence to dry. "My Mom died without a will, so the estate went into Prostate. When it came out all the money stayed with my grandma, cause she's my Mom's mom. Also my Mom and Dad weren't married. They were free spirits. That means they saved lots of money by not getting married. My Dad says that weddings are just huge holes people throw cash into. Which is just stupid. If I had lots of money I wouldn't throw it down a hole. I'd vest it in the sock market. That's what grandma does. My Dad says she's rolling in money. That means she spreads money on the floor and does somersaults on it."

Katie nodded, looking impressed.

Sally waved at her grandmother, who wheeled her horse and trotted over to them.

"Hello, Miss Sally. Would you like to ride Violet here? I've given her a thorough workout, so she's nice and calm."

Bill Hesslop jumped off his hay bale and hurried up to the fence, looking rather alarmed. "I don't think that's such a good idea. Sally, why don't you ride that little pony you were on last time? He's more your speed. He's right over there."

Bill Hesslop pointed to Max, a chubby little Shetland pony who was munching grass in a pasture next to the corral.

"Nonsense, Bill dear," said Mrs. Worthington. "Why, I started riding full-grown horses when I was five. She'll be fine. We'll start slow. Sally dear, come sit up here in front of me."

Mrs. Worthington guided her horse up next to the fence. Sally handed Melvin to Katie and climbed onto the top bar of the fence.

Her grandmother wrapped one arm around Sally's waist and hoisted her into the saddle in front of her. They trotted slowly around the corral, Sally whooping with delight and Bill Hesslop watching nervously. Katie climbed down from the fence and made herself comfortable on a hay bale. She put Melvin on her lap and gave him a good scratch behind the ears. Both of them looked extremely glad they were sitting on a hay bale and not on a horse.

Robbie sat next to them for a while, swinging his chubby legs and chewing on a handful of grass he had yanked up from the pony's pasture, but soon he started to fidget. He climbed down from his hay bale and toddled off toward Max with a determined gleam in his eye. Katie eyed him worriedly, but decided that if she had to choose between watching Melvin and watching Robbie, Melvin was definitely the easier choice.

Max had tired of grass and was ambling over to a pile of sacks bulging with grain which someone had unwisely left in his pasture. With his strong front teeth he tore a hole in one corner of the top sack and a tiny waterfall of grain poured out. As Max indulged himself in this unexpected snack Robbie quietly pulled himself up onto the wobbling pile of grain sacks. He balanced precariously, like a diver on a diving board, then reached out with both hands and awkwardly slid himself stomach first onto the pony's back, where he lay like a very lumpy saddle. Max pulled his nose out of the grain pile in surprise and twisted his head around. He eyed Robbie's rear end curiously, giving a little shake to see if the strange object would fall off. Robbie giggled. Max pricked up his ears at this, deciding this might be a fun game. He started at a slow trot across the pasture. Robbie bounced up and down, laughing hysterically.

Max circled his pasture a few times then headed for the gate, which was closed but not locked. He gave the bars a push with his nose and they were off toward the estate's long gravel drive and freedom.

Behind them footsteps pounded on the gravel. Max sped up, his round belly swaying from side to side. Robbie's giggles got even louder. It looked like the two adventurers were going to pull off their escape into the wide world. But, alas, reality (and a puffing parent) prevailed.

Bill Hesslop ran forward and grabbed Robbie off the pony's back. "That's enough, you two," he said, gasping for air. He set Robbie on his feet and shook his finger at Max. "Max, you should know better. And you, Robbie. With all the dirt and cookies you've managed to tuck away today, all that bouncing is going to make you spew like Old Faithful."

Mrs. Worthington and Sally rode up on Violet. The chestnut mare nickered in a disapproving manner at the pony. Max shook his blond mane at her and began to calmly munch a cluster of dandelions at his feet.

"Oh, I wouldn't worry about our Mr. Robert's digestion," said Mrs. Worthington. "He has a stomach like cast iron. He gets it from his grandpa. That man could eat a five-course Sunday dinner, top if off with three desserts, and then go on the WhirlyGig ride at the State Fair carnival without so much as a twinge of heartburn. Though, I admit he didn't share little Mr. Robert's fondness for soil sampling. You really ought to cure the child of that, Bill dear. I caught him snacking on the compost under my roses the last time he was here. It's a good thing I tell my gardener not to use pesticides."

Bill Hesslop sighed. "Yes, ma'am. I've tried to get Robbie to stop eating dirt. Our doctor says it's just a phase he's going through. He's like a puppy. He'll eat anything. Next he'll probably start chewing on shoes. Well, it's been a pleasure, as always, but we need to get going. I need to get Sally to her school. Her play is tonight and they have one last rehearsal."

"You're coming, right grandma?" said Sally as she slid off of Violet's back. "It's gonna be super terrific. It's about the Pilgrims and the first Thanksgiving. I'm a Squall."

"You mean a Squaw, Sally." said her father.

Sally nodded. "Right. If you're a Naïve American and a girl, then you're a Squall. The boys are Braves, like the baseball team. All the Brownies from my troop are in the play. Course, we don't have boys in the Brownies, so there are some Cub Scouts in the play, but it's still gonna be good."

Mrs. Worthington dismounted. "I'm sure even the Cub Scouts will be unable to dim your thespian brilliance my dear. Of course I'll be there. It will be the highlight of my social season."

End of Excerpt

Made in the USA
Las Vegas, NV
16 July 2022

51707115R00080